THE BLACK CRADLEBOARD

A LAKOTA MYSTERY

Dorothy Black Crow

DOROTHY BLACK CROW

Black Crow Books

Black Crow Books

The Handless Maiden: A Lakota Mystery
Copyright ©2019 by Dorothy Black Crow

All rights reserved.

Cover Design by Nuno Moreira
http://www.nmdesign.org

See more titles by Dorothy Black Crow at
http://dorothyblackcrow.com/

ISBN-13: 978-1-7341597-0-7

Also available in digital formats.

Dedication
to

WARN
Women of All Red Nations
founded by
Lorelei DeCora Means
Madonna Thunderhawk
Phyllis Young

Senator James Abourezk

Bea Medicine
Mary Ann Bear Comes Out
Lee Brightman
Marie Sanchez

Praise for *The Handless Maiden*

"*The Handless Maiden* is not like any mystery you have ever read in your life. It takes place in 1977 on the Lakota Pine Ridge Reservation in the Badlands of South Dakota. Here, the memory of the massacre at Wounded Knee in December, 1890 still burns hot in the tribal memory. Here the ghosts of long dead ancestors are still seen walking in the moonlight. Here there are sweat lodge ceremonies that produce astounding visions. And here, 300 FBI agents have been sent to put down a rebellion by a few dozen young Lakota Warriors and they aren't about to waste their time reading you your rights. Now Tate Turning Hawk, a young woman recently married to a young medicine man and new to the reservation, is led by a ghost she does not believe in to the body of her friend Joanna Joe, brutally murdered and her hands chopped off. The local police and the FBI could care less. Joanna Joe was a trouble maker. It's up to Tate and her medicine man husband, Alex, to bring justice. They go after the killers the Lakota way, the spiritual way. This is one of those timeless books that stands apart, likely to be read and talked about a hundred years from now."

—JAMES N. FREY, author of *How to Write a Damn Good Mystery*

"The Handless Maiden tells the story of a culture and traditions that are being lost to us—a culture of the Native American Lakota— brought to vivid life by Dorothy Mack when the Native American movement fought for justice and the FBI fought for control. Bravo!"

—CARA BLACK, author of 19 Aimee LeDuc Paris mysteries

"This was a powerful story with such beautifully drawn characters and such important themes. With The Handless Maiden, Dorothy Black Crow has produced a no-holds-barred, knock-your-socks-off

v

unforgettable story of the South Dakota Badlands and those who, for centuries, have called it home. Like all classic novels, conflict is at the story's heart—the brutal conflict of cultures, white and red; of the urban Native experience and reservation life; of the world of the flesh and the world of the spirit. Black Crow paints the landscape with lyrical strokes of stunning detail. Her characters speak with authentic voice. Her language is rich and full of the power of truth. And the thread of mystery she's woven into every page is a taut and twisting beauty that will, I guarantee, keep you riveted until the end."

—WILLIAM KENT KRUEGER, author of 18 Cork O'Connor
Minnesota mysteries & *Ordinary Grace*

Acknowledgements

Orpha Berry, Scott Branchfield, Susan Clayton-Goldner, Susan Dominguez, Jean Esteve, Lily Gardner-Butts, Claire Hall, Susan Kelly, Patsy Lally, Sue Lick, Vickie Mazzone, Lloyd Meeker, Martha Miller, Bob Olds, Martha Ragland, Margie Reynolds, Lois Rosen, Leah Schrifter, Dan Stein, Jane Sutherland, Pam Wegner, Theresa Wisner, and lastly, my book designer, Sarah Katreen Hoggatt, and my mentor, James N. Frey.

Disclaimer

My husband Selo Black Crow said if I ever wrote
About the Res, it'd be all lies.

He was right.

This story is Fiction, since the Truth is seldom believable.
Names and places have been changed. However,
check out the References at the end for the
Connie Uri Lawsuit, and continuing atrocities today.

In Memory of

all those ghost children—
never mothers and fathers
never leaders and teachers
never riders and runners
never spoke the language
never walked on the Land
never joined the People

Lakota Words in the Story

FOR READERS to understand how Lakota is spoken, I chose to write out pronunciation rather than to use linguistic symbols, such as č for *ch* or š for *sh* or ġ for *gh*. I also use marks to indicate which syllable is accented. Otherwise, readers might think that *ate* means to have eaten, but *até* means father, or that *ina*, mother, would be pronounced *eye-nah* instead of *iná*. Worse yet, readers might think that *waste* means waste, as in waste time or waste money, but *washté* means good.

Words are listed by frequency in the story and are grouped by type. If used only once or twice, their English meaning follows directly. Sacred words and names are capitalized.

Iná—mother
Até—father
Kolá—friend
Toka—outsider
Hokshila—boy
Hokshicala—baby boy

Ohan—yes
Hiya—no
Washté—good
Shicha—bad
Hau—hello
Pilamaya—thanks
Inachni—hurry up
Wanaghi—ghost
Tun—birth cord
Checkpa Ognake—cord pouch
Woluta—Sacred tobacco tie
Wakan Tanka—the Great Mystery
Wichasha wakan—medicine man
Hanblechia—Vision Quest
Hochoka—Sacred Circle
Inipi—Sacred Sweat Lodge
Chanunpah—Sacred Pipe

Map of South Lakota, Eagle Nest and Camp Crazy Horse

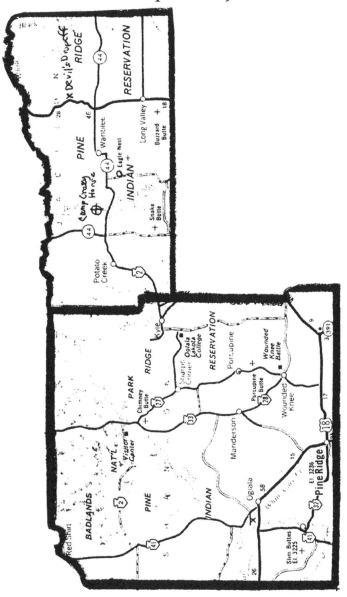

Pine Ridge Res – South Lakota – 1978

Pine Ridge Indian Reservation
May 1977

WE COME from the Great Sioux Nation, the Land of Crazy Horse, Sitting Bull, and Red Cloud. We are descendants of the 1868 Ft. Laramie Treaty with the United States.

For years the U.S. Army fought us. Yet we survived. They took our pony herds and slaughtered the bison. Yet we survived. They took our land and fenced us on Reservations. Yet we survived. They massacred our women and children at Wounded Knee. Yet we survived. Smallpox and Spanish Flu filled our graveyards. Yet we survived.

Boarding Schools took our children away: some remained away in graveyards, others returned tough and cruel. Families were split as Relocation lured our young men to Chicago and Los Angeles for jobs that vanished. Some men slept in alleys or under bridges; most forgot our language, our culture.

On the Reservation, mothers lost their children, taken away for White families to adopt. Other women, who bore only one child or were barren, were pitied as well, since they had no large family. Our wealth is our tribe and our family. We lost a generation of chiefs and warriors.

Yet we survive.

CHAPTER 1
ALEX TURNING HAWK

May 1977
Pine Ridge Reservation, SD
Camp Crazy Horse, midnight

OUR PEOPLE always felt safe on the Res, once we plunged down into Redstone Basin in the Badlands of South Dakota and crossed the White River onto our own land. Even with paint peeling off, our sign said: Land of Red Cloud. No gate, barbed wire, or border guard, just a palpable line, a thickness in the air—safe on our side, danger on the other, where the Kadoka sheriff patrolled Whiteman Law.

But this May night the danger felt closer, some intrusion on Turning Hawk land, danger before dawn in the old log cabin at Camp Crazy Horse. An insistent tap-tap-tap on the thick door woke Alex Turning Hawk, the young medicine man. It could be someone coming for doctoring. He'd have to get dressed, light the lamp, and feed the visitor first.

He reached to hug Tate, her big belly a cocoon for their child, ready to lean over to hear the solid tica-tica-tica of the tiny heartbeat inside, turning his day into a miracle of life. But now her pillow was empty. Empty because his mother, hearing Tate was pregnant, had hauled his wife and her piano into town to be safe with the midwives. Tate had protested, of course, but when Iná said in English, "Barely married and already so big!" he knew better than to oppose his mother. She was on the warpath. Ever since the Great Mystery created the Earth, mothers have had power.

Still, he worried that Tate, surrounded by midwives wearing black in a house full of herbs, would be frightened and lonely. Or worse, she'd defy Iná by going to the Eagle Nest Clinic for checkups and Whiteman medicine.

Tap-tap-tap.

Was Tate in labor, and they'd come to get him? Something worse, a miscarriage? He yanked the door open, stepped into the moonlight and looked around.

No one.

Only the sweetness of chokecherry and wild plum blossoms in the night air. The pile of kindling beside the door lay undisturbed. Then, above him, a flapping of wings. Hawk, his Guardian Spirit, who usually greeted him just before dawn, hovered and circled overhead, calling, "kree–kree." Strange behavior for a night hawk.

He answered, "kree–kree." Something was wrong. He pulled on jeans, flannel shirt, parka, and moccasins. Hawk buzzed him again and flew toward the pines, as if the trouble lay north, where the full moon hovered over the Badlands.

"Kree–kree, kree–kree," floated on the wind. The moon had turned the tall prairie grass to silver and shone on the path to the pines his moccasins knew so well. Walking out onto the land was part of his spiritual practice—We don't own the Land, She owns us—but tonight he felt an urgency of wings.

As he ran past the sweat lodges and Sundance grounds, past the horse corral out north toward the Badlands Wall at the edge of the

Res world, he caught the spring fragrance of sage and horsemint. Below Redstone Basin's maze of barren arroyos twisted and turned out of sight. Purple and indigo shadows shone from the full moonlight. Old bison trails.

Hawk circled above, calling, "kree–kree–" then disappeared down the old trail.

The path to the ancient Vision Cave was familiar. He'd walked it three times as a medicine-man-in-training, fasting for Spirit Power. Few people knew of this sacred place, hidden on a high narrow ledge, dug from Badlands shale a hundred years ago by his Turning Hawk ancestors. Dug into the rock face just big enough for a man to crawl in and pray.

When he reached the ledge, he flinched. His family's rock altar lay strewn about as if a coyote had knocked it over while seeking prey. The white buffalo skull, which usually sat on top of the altar, rested amid scattered small red prayer flags in front of the Vision Cave. Hawk sat on them, silent, as if to say: trouble. Something more than a coyote had been here since he'd fasted here a year ago to become a medicine man.

A musty smell came from the elk hide door flap covering the opening in the rock wall. The slight breeze shifted, carrying the odor of old leather and ashes.

Nothing should be inside.

Lifting the door flap, he anchored it with a rock and crawled into the familiar womb-like cave, his back blocking the moonlight. In the darkness, echoes of ancient fasting songs swirled around him and the air filled with the fragrance of sweetgrass. As his hands swept across the uneven floor, he felt a bundle of leather with a wood frame, which he turned and dragged to the entrance.

Moonlight glittered on the beads of an old cradleboard lying on the rock ledge. It was about two feet long and a foot wide, just the right size to hold a baby wrapped in leather and laced in with thongs. Like a backpack, the wood frame and leather straps let a mother carry her baby on her back, or else she'd hang the cradleboard on a nearby tree. Babies were never left alone. They belonged in tipis and living rooms, held in laps by both men and women, so they could hear the language, the old stories and the laughter. So unlike Tate, raised in a crib with bars, left alone to cry in her own nursery.

As he touched the old cradleboard he felt its coldness in his fingers. Yet it was charred at the edges. Had it been burned in a fire, or merely singed at the edge of a campfire? And the beadwork was odd—pink beads, not the usual sacred colors of red, white, and green. Perhaps the moonlight made it look as if red beads had faded. Then he saw the whole pattern, a Vision Hill design: striped hills in two rows running down each side.

Alex gasped. It was the Turning Hawk design, passed down for generations, the same beaded design on his own cradleboard hanging in Iná's house, waiting to be used for his unborn son. As a baby, Iná had laced him into it so he could watch the old people fill the log cabin where he'd learned to listen to the language. Had this one belonged to a Turning Hawk ancestor? Had it been singed in a prairie fire?

Could this cradleboard and lizard bag, passed down for generations, have been his father's? Had his father Até, gone more than a dozen years, returned in secret and brought this cradleboard as a gift, even though he'd wrecked their altar? Had Hawk seen the man and called Alex to him? He looked out at the buffalo skull, but his Guardian Spirit had flown away.

Turning back to the cradleboard, he found a tiny beaded leather bag tied to one side made to hold a baby's umbilical cord as a connection to Mother Earth. This one was beaded in a faded black-and-white lizard design, meant for a boy. Like his own lizard bag had been beaded by Iná and tied to his cradleboard for protection. But this one was so worn and old, it must have been his father's. Left here to let him know his father was nearby.

He lifted the cradleboard to take it home to show Iná—but maybe not—yet. His thoughts drifted from his mother to his hands. The cradleboard was too heavy to be empty.

Drawn by its fragrance of sweetgrass, Alex lifted the cradleboard's head cover. Moonlight lit the blackened face of a baby, eyes and mouth shut, painted or brushed with ashes. For a moment it looked like the face of a life-size doll, but the powdery smell of powdered yucca root told him: no. Could this baby, hidden and abandoned overnight, still be alive? Lakota medicine men couldn't touch the dead, but he leaned close to the face to listen for a sigh, a breath. None. Not long dead in the cold of the cave.

Had his father brought home a dead baby, another son? No, Até, raised traditionally, could never have blackened a baby's face, let alone a son, even if dead. Or never put it here to desecrate Turning Hawk land. No, someone had found a Turning Hawk cradleboard and used it to terrify his family—Tate and his unborn son. A cold wind blew along the ledge, chilling him. Thankfully Tate was safe in town, guarded by Iná and her midwives.

Then he noticed what looked like a black snake around the neck, but more like a Catholic rosary with black beads strung by hand. Moonlight shone on them, revealing a string of black cloth prayer ties—the opposite of red prayer ties filled with sacred tobacco for protection. This cradleboard was a hex. He scrambled backwards to get away from them, each tie full of black prayers for him and his family.

The black ties glowed in the moonlight and grew bigger and closer, as if they could reach out and push him into the rough stone walls. He'd never seen Black Medicine before, only heard stories of misfortune laid on families who had suddenly disappeared. If only he'd brought his sacred pipe along, with matches and *kinnick-kinnick* to smoke out evil.

All he carried was his song for strength and courage. He stood up, taller now, his head scraping the top of the cave, and sang the prayer over and over, starting with a high wail and descending into a deep bass groan: "*Tunkashila, unshimalaye.* Grandfather, take pity on me. Take pity on my family, Tate and Iná and my unborn son. As his voice filled the Vision Cave and echoed out into the night, his fear left and he sang from his heart, for Até-wherever-he-was.

And for the dead baby lying before him. From his parka pocket he unsheathed his knife, knelt down and cut the black ties loose from the baby's neck, lifting them by the blade and flinging them over the ledge into the chasms of the Badlands darkness below. Then, with his neckerchief he wiped the blackness from the baby's face and sat next to him. All people were *unshika*, he knew, pitiful in the eyes of the Great Mystery, especially this abandoned, lost baby.

"Kree–kree–" he cried out into the night, calling his Spirit Power to help him. Then he pulled the cradleboard into his lap and sang the words that opened the way into the Spirit World, "*Kola le-che-e-chu—*" Even a dead baby, lost in the Spirit World, might hear, might sense cries or tears. He would call to the dead baby and find him.

He crooned to the baby who had a small bump of a hawk-nose like himself. "*Hokshicala!* Little-one, you will never be alone here, but with the ancestors. Little-one, I cannot touch you but I can pray for you. I will help you find your family who will care for you."

He rocked the cradleboard and asked: "Did your mother abandon you to die? Who found you and laced your tiny hands into your cradleboard? Who dressed you in soft buckskin? Who closed your eyes, your mouth, your hands and feet? Who painted your face black and wound black tobacco ties around your neck?"

In the Spirit World there were no answers. His Turning Hawk ancestors spun around him in a whirlwind, outraged by the violence and death that had entered their sacred space. For them he must purify it and rebuild the sacred altar—or else it would be haunted forever, and no one would come to fast and pray.

At last Alex returned to the Ordinary World, where nothing made any sense. Only that someone had sent evil into the most sacred Turning Hawk place, out to destroy him, his mother Iná, his wife Tate, and his unborn child. Were they safe in town?

Was this an omen? That he and Tate's baby would die? Or was it a threat? Whose baby? Sick or killed? Dead how long? Why hide him here? Who else knew of this sacred place? Who else had a Turning Hawk cradleboard? His heart skipped a beat. Had Até, his father, gone for so many years, returned now? All he remembered was riding horsie on Até's knee and being tossed in the air to reach the sky. Could Até be the father of this *hokshicala*, who might be his brother?

No—even Até, who gave up his medicine power for a woman, wouldn't bring evil on himself and pollute the Turning Hawk Vision Cave. Yet his father might be nearby, watching. No wonder Hawk, his Guardian Spirit, had flown to wake him and lead him to the Vision Cave.

Wherever his father might be, the *hokshicala* couldn't be left in the Badlands. He'd bring the old Turning Hawk cradleboard to Iná, who might know secrets hidden in the Spirit World.

As he left, he found a footprint in the dust of the ledge. He measured his cowboy boots against the work boot print. Size ten, his own size and weight. Not a cowboy, who'd wear boots with pointy toes and heels to stay in the stirrup. Not a rancher, perhaps a hired hand.

Somehow he'd have to carry the *hokshicala* away from the Vision Cave, come back and purify it later. Where could he take him? Bury the baby somewhere in the Badlands? Someone had cared enough to bead a lizard bag for him, even if it hadn't been enough protection. He could turn him in to the Eagle Nest Tribal police. But rumors on the Res spread like wildfire: a dead baby left in the Badlands, and worse, in Turning Hawk's Vision Cave. He had to keep this desecration of Turning Hawk land a secret while searching for the person who had stolen or killed the *hokshicala*. Of the remaining Turning Hawks, only his mother Iná had a strong enough heart to help. Furious as she'd be at the threat to the family, she'd keep quiet and wait. She would recognize the old-style cradleboard and must have heard the story of its rescue from fire. And since she was a midwife who both brought people into this world and took them out of it, she'd know what to do with the *hokshicala*, maybe even determine cause of death. Families stood together in times of trouble. She'd know what to do, maybe even know who was out to destroy their family. Fortunately, she rose even earlier than him.

Gently he loosened the elk hide door flap and wrapped the cradleboard and baby in it. He held the bundle awkwardly in his arms, slipping silently through the spring prairie grass so he wouldn't be seen. Past the horse corral, past the AIM warriors sleeping at Camp Crazy Horse among the tipis and sundance grounds. No time to leave a note. Smokey, his second in command, could run things until he returned. They'd think a visitor had come in the middle of the night to get Alex for an emergency doctoring.

His neckerchief fell off, but he didn't stop until he reached his pickup. He slid the cradleboard onto the passenger side. As he drove by moonlight in low gear out to the road, he searched for a name. Naming was crucial. Any native person, especially a medicine man, would give an unknown dead baby a name so it could enter the Spirit World.

He spoke to the dead baby in the cradleboard on the car seat near his knee, "Hokshicala, maybe Iná will know who you are and what to do."

CHAPTER 2
TATE

Eagle Nest Housing, midnight

TATE TURNING Hawk couldn't sleep. She lay awake in her bedroom at the back of Iná's Midwife House in Eagle Nest. Her hands cuddled her big belly while she felt her unborn baby's heartbeat. Uncomfortable as it was to sleep on her side, she didn't care.

Back when she and Alex had gone to the Eagle Nest Clinic, she'd heard the stethoscope miracle: a fast tiny tica-tica-tica that made her baby real. Two hearts beating in the same body. She was not alone after all. She'd found a new name for herself: Tate Two Hearts and had told him so. She was strong. She was powerful. She could do anything. Pregnancy was not an illness, but a strength. Her woman's body had created a miracle. Did other pregnant women feel this way? No man ever had two hearts! Alex was more fascinated with the stethoscope, turning it this way and that, figuring out how the tubes connected to the ears so he could make one for himself.

But her life had changed in that moment. Never again would she feel powerless around her mother-in-law, with her hawk eye and jutting jaw. And there she was, Iná screaming again—she listened to

the piercing wails—and the thrum of a pickup engine. In the middle
of the night, could Alex have come into town and Iná caught him
before he could climb in her back bedroom window? But Alex always
turned off the engine before coasting silently into Iná's driveway.
Something else this time. She stumbled out of bed, eager to see Alex,
even if Iná was whacking him with her diamond willow cane.

CHAPTER 3

ALEX

On the road to Eagle Nest Housing, after midnight

NO ONE else was on the road in the dead of night. Eagle Nest loomed like a ghost town, dark and silent. He drove slowly like a drunk sneaking back from an off-Res bar, hoping not to be seen. He knew the streets by heart, diving past the closed gas station and Post Office, deserted log cabins and shacks, darkened missionary houses and bootlegger trailers, past the leaking water tower and college center trailer. Only one yard light glowed from afar in front of the cinder-block tribal police station.

He turned into the Bureau of Indian Affairs housing circle with its street lights shot out months ago. The prefabs huddled together on the land like prairie dogs braving the north wind. Halfway around the circle he turned off the engine and coasted into the driveway to his mother's house. It looked just like the others, set on a half basement with steps up the first floor, except that Iná's yard was uncluttered by broken-down cars or washing machines. Even this early the kitchen light was on. Old timers rose before dawn, preparing for the day.

Before he could get out, her kitchen door opened and there she stood in her apron with her doughy hands grasping her diamond willow cane, ready to whip any intruder. In the olden days men carved diamond-shaped holes from a thick willow branch for a cane as a sign of authority as well as a crutch. Chief Turning Hawk had given his to his daughter Iná before he died, since she was now head of the family and needed protection. Hah. The cane hadn't protected Alex.

It was her strength and her weakness. She wasn't lame, she was bossy. He'd heard women in town talk behind her back—"who does she think she is, thumping that cane as if ruling a kingdom?" But he didn't care. He was proud of her. She'd always told him, "You and I are the only Traditionals left." No one else in Eagle Nest had one. And she used it well—limped in front of strangers, thumped for attention in town meetings, beat rascally boys and mangy dogs, and threatened anyone in her way.

She clomped down the cement steps, dusted her hands off on her apron and came near. Frowning, she said, "*Itéshni, Mato Chikila*?" What's wrong, Little Bear?

His childhood name. As soon as Tate and he had a son, Iná would have to stop using it. He opened the pickup door and said in a low voice, "*Mielo*, Alex." It's me, Alex. He couldn't bring the bundle in. Full of death, it would contaminate Iná's house.

He took her arm and led her around the pickup to the passenger side. Hokshicala needed to be treated with care. The yard light barely shone into the front seat. She peered in. "Middle of the night, you bring me old hide to repair? Or my grandson's cradleboard?"

She looked so expectant. Of course he hadn't finished it, but he still had time before his son was born. This was a very different cradleboard lying in his pickup. He blocked the door handle with his body. Not a good idea to come to her after all. If only he'd known which cop was on duty, a traditional, who would understand the situation, or a modern officer ready to blame him, he'd have gone to the cops directly. "Something I found in the Vision Cave. *Tawachin shicha.*" Something bad. As soon as he said it, he knew he couldn't shove her away.

She pushed him aside and yanked the pickup door open. The overhead light shone down on the wrapped bundle. She reached in, brushed aside the old hide, and stared at the cradleboard. Then she fingered the beadwork strips. She must have recognized the Turning Hawk design because she said, "Pink beads. Sloppy work. Careless, let it get burned. Very old."

She stood back up and faced him. "You didn't guard the Turning Hawk Vision Cave? You let someone steal from a museum and hide it like a cache?"

Before he could stop her, she turned back to the cradleboard and lifted the head flap. As if the cradleboard held a ghost come alive, Hokshicala's face floated up to her. He hadn't wiped off all the black paint, but at least the black tobacco ties were gone.

Her hand froze in the air while her mouth choked off a high loud wail, and she fell back against him, her body rigid as stone. More wails filled the predawn air. He caught her and turned her around, shocked to see her face white as her apron, her eyes empty as she swayed against him. He steadied her and felt her throat for a pulse. Heart attack or stroke? Some memory had taken her breath away, stopped her heart for a moment. In that instant his mother turned old and frail, bent over some sad past event. He'd never seen her so frightened, so ghostly white. The cradleboard had brought her memories of evil misfortune alive.

He'd been fearful of the bundle desecrating the sacred Turning Hawk Vision Cave, but Iná seemed to be frightened of something else. Was it the dead baby? The burned cradleboard? The Turning Hawk beaded design? She must have seen the cradleboard before.

She must know who had made it. Maybe she even suspected whose baby this was. His father, Até?

He'd ask, but he knew she wouldn't say. The elders wouldn't talk about the starvation days when they were shoved onto the Reservation, not allowed to hunt, separated from their families and beaten at boarding schools. They kept their lives private.

He held his mother in his arms until her shaking stopped. "Why would anyone leave a dead baby in the Vision Cave just before I go fasting? Who is out to get me? It can't be Até."

Iná replied, "Maybe not just you, maybe threaten my grandson."

CHAPTER 4
TATE

Iná's Midwife House, after midnight

TATE RAN to the kitchen door and opened it.

Alex, on the other side of their pickup, called out, "Don't come down."

So what if she wore only her baggy nightgown that didn't hide the bulge of her belly. It was dark out. Her husband and her mother-in-law were at it again, and with her new power, she'd help Alex. "What's the matter with Iná?" she asked as she ran down the steps toward their pickup. "Did she catch you?"

Iná, shaking her cane, said, "Go inside. You can't come near."

She was supposed to stay inside. Play the piano, give lessons to the kids in town. Sew beadwork. Weave baskets. Soften hides. Brew herbs. She wanted to be out in the country with Alex, picking sweetgrass and wild plums—yet here he was, backing her onto the kitchen steps.

Alex looked at her feet. "Get shoes on." Then he added, "Pregnant women cannot be near dead babies, for fear the dead will spirit your unborn baby away."

He already knew she didn't believe in the old superstitions. She put her hands on her belly. "You really believe that? You think I'm not able to protect my baby?"

"Our baby." A deep frown crossed his face. "It's happened before."

She pushed past him to peer into the pickup. Only an old elk hide on the seat, and Iná, flailing her arms on the far side. "What dead baby?"

No use telling Alex to ignore his mother. So they wanted her protected. She ran back inside to get her moccasins. Then she invaded Iná's room—normally not allowed—and put on her mother-in-law's black oilcloth butchering apron and worn leather gloves. Her new regalia. At the top of the steps she announced, "Ready." But they didn't notice her.

Alex had walked around to his mother's side. They were still flinging Lakota at each other. But she was Tate Two Hearts. She bounded down the steps and climbed into the driver's side of the pickup. She slid to the center and pulled the bulky leather bundle onto the apron in her lap. So this was the "dead baby"? She lifted the hide and saw a charred wood frame laced with leather, like the cradleboard she was making for her baby, just like Alex's hanging in Ina's bedroom. Then she saw, sewn onto leather, two strips of old red-white-green beads.

Even though faded, she recognized Alex's Turning Hawk design. Surely this was what they were arguing about: a family cradleboard. "Is the dead baby inside?" she said aloud.

Then they noticed her, gloves and all. They looked past her, beyond to the open kitchen door, its light shining out into the darkness. Oh, no, another mistake. Yet with the bundle in her lap, she could hardly get out to close the door before some neighbor nearby woke up and saw.

Before Iná could open her mouth, Alex said, "Stay put, Tate. I'll shut it in a minute." He lowered his hand, their signal for her to let him handle his mother.

Still outside the pickup, Iná leaned in and glared at her. "Too stupid to be brave, you going to kill my grandson inside you." Then Iná put her hand on her heart as if it were hurting.

Alex lifted Iná into the passenger side, along with her cane. "Not now, Question Box. It's my mother's heart." His face looked tight with worry. He closed the passenger door, then closed the kitchen door, got into the driver's side, and started the pickup.

Iná pushed her over towards Alex. "You lean on your elbows, you squash dead baby in that cradleboard."

It *was* crowded in the pickup. Tate quit trying to undo the hide to see the dead baby and sat up, squeezing her arms to her sides, but still holding the bundle in her hands. She said slowly, "I am holding a dead baby. We must take it to the cops at the substation."

Iná cried, "We not going to Pine Ridge BIA law, we keep Turning Hawk Honor."

What was Turning Hawk Honor? Keeping silent, hiding a crime?

As Alex backed out of the driveway he shifted away from her so she had room for her arms. He gave her that secret smile that said everything would be okay. As he headed out of the housing circle, he said, "We're taking Iná to the IPH clinic first."

Was Iná really having a heart attack? Or just arguing as usual?

Iná shrieked. "Not going to die. Not before I see my grandson grow up." Her fierce face had returned. Her lips pulled down over sharp teeth.

"What about your heart?" Alex asked.

"Recovered." Iná hit her chest, flour dusting the air. "Hurry up. Turn around."

Her mother-in-law had a hard heart and a fierce love—not for her, but for Alex.

"Pretty soon light," Iná said. "No cops. No BIA papers. No Moccasin Telegraph. Drive on to my church. We going to a safe place. Only I got the keys."

That meant the keys to the Episcopal Church, which Iná helped clean every Saturday.

Then Iná said to her in English, "Okay, Question Box. You want to be midwife. Since you don't believe in power of dead baby around pregnant woman, I let you help."

Iná must have changed her mind, thinking that Tate was too afraid to touch the dead, and would refuse. Hah. She did want to be a midwife, wanted to learn about birthing the Indian way, and to prepare for her own birthing as well. Still, this training would be different: preparing the dead for burial. But she had to start sometime. Even though she knew you never said thank you, you just accepted a gift in silence, she said to Iná, "I want to learn women's work." That should stop her badgering.

Iná replied, "Not much help now, you so pregnant, baby almost popping out."

In spite of the darkness, Tate recognized the white clapboard one-story building with high narrow windows on each side: the Eagle Nest Episcopal Church. A dozen steps led up to the double doors. She'd not been inside, but Alex had told her it was plain: no stained glass, rough wooden benches and a simple cross at the altar. Built in the olden days when the Government forced people to become either Catholic or Episcopal in order to get beef issue rations. Pine Ridge got the Holy Rosary Mission and Eagle Nest got an Episcopal Church where the Turning Hawks were buried in its cemetery. Alex parked behind the church near the outhouse so they wouldn't be seen.

Iná climbed out, shook her cane and pointed her chin at the dark gray sky to the east.

That meant: look, dawn was coming soon.

Alex opened his door and said, "The last time I been inside was at Grandpa Turning Hawk's wake and funeral: upstairs for the services, downstairs for the food."

Downstairs was also where the midwives worked to prepare a body for a four-day wake and funeral.

"Don't mind Iná," Alex said. "Hand me the bundle. It's my responsibility. I found Hokshicala in the Vision Cave."

Clutching the bundle tighter, Tate whispered. "This is women's work. You're supposed to stay outside and guard the door."

Iná poked her head back inside. "Hurry up, you two." Using her cane, she hooked Tate and the cradleboard out of the pickup, dragged Tate around the side of the church, down the cement steps, and opened the basement door with her key.

Tate stumbled into the total darkness within and bumped into a bench. It was cold, and the basement had no windows.

Iná flicked on the lights. "Shut the door. No one will care that we down here."

Blinded by the bare bulbs overhead, Tate looked around at the low-ceilinged room lined with folding chairs and tables stacked against the opposite cement wall. Cooking pots hung on a far wall in the kitchen, blocked off by a built-in serving table.

Bookcases filled with black Bibles and Hymnals—in Lakota, she guessed. On the opposite wall hung a carved figure of Jesus on a wooden cross. No cradleboard for Jesus. Still, He might help. They needed all the help they could get from anyone's God.

"Alex?" Iná asked. "Where is he? Tell him to get in here!"

"Doesn't he have to stay out?"

"*Hiya.*" No. "We need him to carry the smudge pot and sage. Men's work to purify this basement, so we work in safety."

And guard the door. Tate reached out behind her to close the basement door. Alex stood there in the light, carrying his sacred pipe bag, smudge pot and branches of sage.

"My son, so slow tonight," Iná said, and then laughed. "He fast enough, other times."

Of course Alex didn't want to be there, to watch the examination of a dead baby. To him it wasn't a dead baby, but a person. She'd already heard him calling it Hokshicala.

Behind her Alex shut the solid basement door.

Iná pointed her lips toward a serving table by the kitchen. "Over there."

Tate walked over and laid the bundle on the table.

"Now he smudge us, then purify room, stay back in corner and pray. That way we safe from death. He purify the room, smoke out bad spirits." Iná handed Alex her worn lighter to ignite the sage in the smudge pot.

Alex blew on the leaves and twigs until the fragrant smoke rose in the air. He grabbed the handle and waved the smudge pot over the bundle, then let the smoke surround and purify all.

Iná whisked Alex away to the door. He began singing a doleful song, not a lullaby but a mourning song. Tate noticed how he paced back and forth by the basement door, probably wanting to escape, maybe willing the door to open on its own. It was as if Iná had tethered her son inside, keeping his power near enough so they could examine the baby in safety. Tate knew he didn't want to watch them examine the baby's chest, stomach, legs, feet, but as a medicine man, he had to stay to protect them.

Then Iná turned to Tate. "You a piano teacher. Now you want to be midwife?"

Tate nodded. Why not be both midwife *and* concert pianist? She could do both, no problem. After all, her foster father, a doctor, had combined medicine with music.

"*Washté.*" Good. I need a daughter to pass on midwife skills and herbs, birth and death."

She added, "Since you wear apron, you start today. Turn around. I braid your hair—"

Tate jerked away. "No one touches my hair," she cried. Not since her foster mother had tried yanking her hair once when she was small. Only Alex. And now, his mother?

Iná laughed. "Not since Alex, for sure. Now I make single braid down your back, out of way, like grown women do." When Iná finished, she walked around to the opposite side of the table. "Still in nightgown, you want to see what's inside?"

Yes, she still wore her nightgown. And over it, Iná's black butchering apron, supposedly to protect the live baby inside her. She wasn't afraid: she was Tate Two Hearts, strong in her power to create life. And she was born curious. She drew back the elk hide wrapping, revealing for the first time under the bare light bulbs the ancient sparkle of the cradleboard's beaded strips. A head flap covered where a baby's face would be.

"Eh-eh-eh, don't touch," Iná muttered, then spoke in phrases. "Cradleboard. Old style. Black Eyes Camp. Old pink beadwork." As she peered closer, she added, "My grandma would never use them beads, not a warrior color."

"How can you tell it's Black Eyes Camp?" Tate asked. She could smell sage as Alex brushed up behind her and looked at the cradleboard.

He said, "Those beads have faded to pink, but the Vision Hill red-white-black beadwork is our own Turning Hawk design."

"No," said Iná. "Some of that pink stuff is still in the off-Res Martin Bank in display cases behind glass." Iná's voice sounded remote and disapproving as she hovered over the cradleboard, refusing to acknowledge their Turning Hawk design.

"Does pink mean it's a girl's cradleboard?" Tate asked Iná.

Alex flicked the lighter flame, touched the sage in the smudge pot, and guided the smoke downward onto the cradleboard. "Had to be for a boy," he said, "because of the green-and-black beaded lizard bag." Then he asked Iná, "Which ancestor belonged to this cradleboard?"

Iná shook her head. Silence. Finally, she said, "Maybe someone steal it from a museum."

Tate reached out to touch the small leather bag tied to the top of the cradleboard. "So is there a boy doll inside the beaded lizard bag?" she asked.

"Question Box, you too much trouble." Iná pulled the beaded bag away and lifted the leather head flap to reveal a face.

Alex drew back and whispered, "Hokshicala, at last I see your face clearly. A fullblood, with black hair and a bump of a hawk nose, looking like one of us."

"*Hiya,*" Iná cried. "Lotsa hawk nose babies—Swift Hawk, Eagle Hawk, Yellow Hawk, Hawk Wing. Means nothing, Go stand by door while we women find out how baby died."

Tate swayed for a moment. The baby's face was pale and puffy, smudged with dirt on the cheeks and forehead. In his round face the closed eyes were set far apart, the closed lips almost purple, thin and lifeless. Black hair covered his head. He smelled of talcum powder, musty but fragrant, so he must have died recently.

She reached underneath the apron to feel her own live baby, solid, just moving slightly, as if to adjust a leg or arm against her stomach. Baby Two Hearts was fine.

Yet this baby Alex called Hokshicala was not fine.

"You want to see dead baby?" Iná asked. "I let you untie it."

As Tate clumsily untied the cradleboard lacing, some strips broke loose as the old leather crumbled. Then she pulled the beaded leather strips aside.

Beneath lay a naked baby. Tiny delicate hands, smaller than her little finger, lay next to his body. Pale blue fingernails tiny as glass beads. Poor baby. He hadn't even been laid on cotton padding in a soft gown—which might have had an embroidered name. Perhaps his body would show some identifying mark. Even with gloves on, she felt his skin cold to the touch.

"*Hnnn,*" Iná muttered. Her frown meant: Don't ask. Instead she said, "You keep gloves on, I not need them. Touching dead babies don't matter to me, old with no more children. I show you how to examine."

Tate looked up from the table to Iná's slightly wrinkled face. Today she looked almost frail. Even though Iná didn't really like her—Tate wasn't the wife Iná had chosen for Alex—she wasn't being deliberately cruel, hoping that Tate would miscarry. She was just old and burdened with responsibilities, worried that her unborn grandson might be harmed. No wonder she clung to her only son. She was just putting Tate through another test.

Iná examined the body closely, touching each part. "Not dead long. One, maybe two days," she said in a flat voice.

Tate bent over the dead baby. "How can you tell?"

"Body stiff few hours after death. Then, see, body go limp."

Tate saw how gently Iná lifted each limp arm and hand, looking for injuries. Bending each leg at the knee and ankle, then gently laying them back down. "Bones working. Nothing broken here. Also, skin pale. No blood flowing now." Iná's hands moved up to the swollen belly. "But not a blue baby. Chest normal, lungs empty. *Chekpa ognake*"—Iná hesitated, looked around. "Where that lizard bag?"

Chekpa ognake? Was that Lakota for the baby's small shriveled penis? The knotted belly button? No, Iná was waving her hand at the small bag with a black-and-green beaded lizard on it. Tate untied it from the top of the cradleboard and handed it to Iná.

"A boy," she confirmed. Iná opened the pouch and shook it loose. Nothing came out. "Ay-ee!" she cried. "No birth cord. No protection.

Now we know why this baby don't survive. Mother don't believe, or hospital doctors throw cord away."

All of a sudden Tate could see Iná hovering over her when baby Turning Hawk would be born, then cutting the cord and putting a part of it into a beaded bag. And she understood in that instant *why* Iná had been insisting that Tate bead a tiny lizard bag, not one with a turtle design—without saying so, Iná wanted a grandson.

Tate was sure the heart beating inside her belly was a girl. She asked Iná, "So he wasn't protected. But what did he die of?"

"Hard to say how he die." Iná brushed the tiny neck and face with her hand. "No red spots—measles, smallpox—no bruises, no broken bones. But on face, Badlands ground-up paint." Her voice continued, steady and even as she gently pushed open the baby's eyes. "Maybe, hnnnn, tiny red dots, burst blood vessels. Choked out or smothered?" Iná checked the neck again and motioned to Tate to look. "No bruises on neck. Baby not strangled. Maybe smothered."

Tate flinched. Iná must have seen dead babies before, choked or smothered. How hard that must have been. Tears filled her eyes. All this learning about babies' bodies was for nothing. This baby didn't just die, he hadn't been wanted. She uttered one of the few Lakota words she'd learned: "*Unshika.*" Pitiful.

"*Unshika,*" repeated Iná, then paused, and looked down. "We wrap him at least." She ran into the kitchen, opened a drawer, and brought back a white linen tablecloth.

Together they unfolded the soft cloth, slid it under the body, and tucked in the feet, arms and head. Tate, on her side, felt something behind the neck, reached under, and clumsily held up a tiny dirty rag.

"Eh-eh-eh," Iná shook her head and grabbed the remnant from Tate's gloved hand. "*Shicha, shicha,*" she cried, dropped it on the floor, and stomped on it as if it were alive.

Shicha meant bad, very bad. It looked like a faded prayer tie. Had someone prayed for the dead baby? Prayed for it to die?

"Quick," Iná said to Tate, her foot still pressed heavily on the tie. "Quick, lace up dead body into cradleboard." Then she called out, "You by door, bring smudge, bring spade."

Alex lit the smudge pot again, blowing on the flame, and waved the sage smoke over the whole table, intoning, "Smudge this empty bag, this empty body."

Iná released her foot. "Now scoop up this *insect* and burn it."

It wasn't an insect. "What is it?" asked Tate.

Alex sighed, signaling with his hands that meant he'd explain later. "Bad medicine. One last black tobacco tie." He carried a spade from the closet by the door, slid the flattened cloth into the smudge pot, and watched the dried tobacco sputter.

Tate got it. Black medicine, Ju-ju. Left for them to find. She'd heard the superstition.

Iná said, "Best to burn 'em, not bury 'em. Black curses could poison the ground. Turning Hawk ground." Iná peered at the dead baby. "Old jealousies."

Old jealousies, what could they be? Tate stopped at the sight of Iná's face. Tears streaked down her cheeks. Between her flat calm words, she'd been crying silently. Tate took her mother-in-law's hands in her own, felt in them the tremor of some unknown loss, as if Iná had seen a ghost from long ago.

CHAPTER 5
ALEX

Episcopal Cemetery, after midnight

IN THE olden days the Government forbid us to bury our dead out on our own land, wrapped in a buffalo hide on a red scaffold. As a child when Alex had seen Grandpa Turning Hawk lifted high on a platform of tree branches painted red, he was warned never to tell. Now everyone made do with plots in a row in the little fenced cemetery above the church.

Alex opened the basement door and tossed the smoldering tobacco tie into a trash bin. "Iná, it's almost getting light. We—"

"*Wana*." Now, Iná replied. She'd dried her tears. She turned off the lights, shoved his wife with the bundled cradleboard out, and locked the basement door. "Time to bury."

He caught Tate before she stumbled over the spade on the concrete steps. "Hokshicala isn't ready to be buried," he said to Iná. "He's a person, and we don't even know his name."

Iná snapped her eyes at him—that fierce look. "Silence. No talk, now we outside."

"We have to talk, Iná," Tate whispered. "You can't just bury a dead body. You have to report the crime to the police."

Iná grabbed the bundle from Tate, and with her cane started up the steps. "No cops. No Moccasin Telegraph. Best in ground, buried." "And I say no burial!" Alex took Tate's hands before she could grab Hokshicala back. They were standing in such a small space, it would be easy to start shoving each other. He said to Iná, "First, we Turning Hawks must find out who he is. Then he can be buried in our plot."

Iná glared at him, clutching the bundle tightly. She switched to Lakota. "Never. I the elder. You not. You bring it to me, midwife. I find what happened. Smothered out. By someone not us. Now you bring spade. I carry dead baby. I bury dead baby. So no one knows. Decided."

From the olden days sons honored their mothers, the stronghold of extended families like clans. They carried the knowledge and wisdom of the tribe, its traditions and history, to pass on to keep the people strong.

He couldn't swing the spade and hit her, but he could wrest the bundle from her. And then what? Dishonor Motherhood? He'd defied her once before, in Minneapolis, by marrying Tate rather than his mother's reservation choice. But here, now, in Iná's territory, two against one didn't matter. He hugged Tate and whispered in her ear, "later."

Iná carried the bundle up the cement steps and onto the path to the cemetery.

Carrying the spade, he and Tate followed her up the hill to the iron gate. Tate walked beside him like a loyal wife, even though he knew she didn't want to. It was still two against one, both as reluctant witnesses.

Beyond them moonlight shone on the mounds of grass and rows of white wooden crosses. Along the back fence chokecherry bushes were in full bloom, filling the night air with sweetness. Near them prairie dogs had dug a warren of holes, leaving moist earth upturned in the lawn. Which meant coyotes nearby. He listened for rustling in the nearby brush, but Iná's determined steps must have driven them away. The cemetery was a place for the living as well as the dead. He reached out for Tate's hand.

Iná jiggled the rusty latch of the gate with its ornate ironwork design.

Tate muttered, "How can you dig a grave in the dark when you can't even see?"

"Close mouth," replied Iná. "I see well enough. I know where to dig." She used her cane to open the gate—creak, creak—and went in.

Tate hesitated, standing back and kicking her moccasins in the dirt. "Alex, I don't like graveyards. I got scared one Halloween. We were playing kick the can, and when I found a big gravestone to hide behind, someone had painted my name on it."

"Few of us can afford a gravestone," Alex said. "Here it's just white crosses." He led Tate inside and closed the gate—more creaks— behind them.

"I'm not going to watch," Tate said. He saw her body stiffen and her face tighten. He knew she was angry, but was trying to keep it inside, no longer trying to argue.

He wasn't sure where Iná was heading, but she led them toward the Turning Hawk plot in the far northwest corner. As they drew near, he saw he wouldn't need the spade. Next to the Turning Hawk white crosses, but outside the plot, a small rectangular hole had already been dug in the earth. He looked at his mother's sad face. He'd spent all his life with her, knew her moods and temperament. But now, she'd kept hidden a secret sorrow. She'd made him carry the spade, so she couldn't have known this hole was waiting. And yet, she hadn't seemed surprised. She'd just stared at it in silence, waiting for him and Tate to catch up.

How much of her early life had his mother hidden from him? Lakota children didn't ask their parents questions about their early life. That was private. If they did, they'd get no answer. Only by staying with an Uncle or Auntie or distant cousin could we wheedle out information about our mother or father's life before we were born.

When Tate saw the hole, she wailed.

Iná raised her cane to strike her. "You not see this. Turn your back. Zip your mouth."

"It's wrong. I'll have no part in this." Tate looked at Alex with a silent question, then said, "I'm gone." She ran back, opened the gate—creak, creak—and stumbled down the path.

He knew it was wrong, too, but saying so out loud would only set Iná off more. He watched Tate turn away. He wanted to go with her. She might stumble over graves or the grass in the dark. He worried that Tate was so stubborn, she might walk back home alone, and someone out late would see her and wonder. But she walked steadily down to the pickup and climbed in. He still had the keys. She might get cold in the pre-dawn chill, but he trusted her to find the old blanket behind the seat. She should sleep, their baby needed rest. He wanted to be with her, but had to stay with his mother, witness to whatever she had in mind. He held the spade like a crutch.

Now that they were alone, Alex switched to Lakota and stared into his mother's eyes. "You knew this hole was here already. You didn't need me to dig it. Is this for Até's baby?"

Iná flinched and backed away. "Quit leaning on spade, maybe you break it. Até is dead."

He'd never believed it, waiting for Até to return, who'd left long ago with Relocation to the big cities with a new woman. He must have come back. She must have guessed who'd dug the grave, yet been embarrassed that his father had returned without her knowing it.

Abruptly Iná dropped the bundle into the grave and tapped the spade. "Cover up grave."

He stood aside. As a small child, he remembered his father's face: not blackened or scarred, just faint and frowning, and then gone. His mother was asking him to hide something in her past. Like covering up a crime. Or an old sorrow. Could the cradleboard have been his father's? Had Até been laced in it when it was singed? Was it even older? Had his grandmother fled a prairie fire? Or a massacre?

Iná had told him he'd had no brothers or sisters, said that the Turning Hawk line ended with him. But if it was a Turning Hawk baby laced in the old cradleboard, could Hokshicala be his father's child? He asked her the easiest of his questions, "Did my grandma *Unchi* make this cradleboard?"

Iná turned her back to him and kicked dirt into the grave. Finally she said, "Dead don't bury the dead. Only we the living."

Indian way, the only son must obey. Yet it was useless trying to bury the past. Reluctantly he shoveled loose dirt on top and smoothed it into a small mound.

"Pound it down flat."

"No," he replied. Let Hokshicala be smothered, stomped on? He wouldn't do it, couldn't stop his mother from doing it, but he could rescue the dead baby later. Hokshicala wasn't just a small dead body, a non-person, maybe even a relative. He'd heard of people dancing on graves, but never stomping on Mother Earth as if to erase it all.

When he didn't move, she threw down her cane and jumped on the grave with her solid black brogans until the dirt flattened. His mother, who'd nearly had a heart attack earlier, bristled with energy. How could a dead baby drive her to such fury? It must be the Turning Hawk beadwork on the old cradleboard.

He dropped the spade and pulled her off the trampled earth.

Panting, she pushed away his arms and said, "No marker. Dig up grass over there." She pointed to the weeds along the fence. "Enough to cover it."

He'd seen it before, his mother on the warpath. On the Res, reputation was all. Forget the Eagle Nest Law and Order Board he was on, forget their own police motto: Protect and Serve. Remember only, First: Honor your Mother. He had no choice. He'd obey, and carry this secret guilt until he himself searched the Res for the baby killer.

He picked up the spade, dug out a clump of grass and carried it to her.

Calm now, she knelt and brushed the grass over the dirt until it blended in. Her hands fluttered over the grave like a benediction. She mumbled something—a prayer or a curse? Wind swept through the cemetery, whisking away her words.

Then they stood, still at odds, he opposite his mother, who leaned on her cane, breathing heavily. In the cool spring night air, he listened to the south wind whistle through the Episcopal cemetery. It blew against their legs and back, whipped Iná's floury apron and his parka, but left the bundle underground where no wind could sweep it away.

At last Iná brushed her hands on her apron, and flashed her eyes at him. She stumbled as she tapped his spade. "Say nothing."

Silence hovered over the town of Eagle Nest. Only those in the Spirit World knew of the double desecration, first in the Vision Cave, and now, in the Episcopal cemetery.

Was she ill? Her heart? Alex grabbed his mother's arm and walked her to the pickup. He said, "Now we have to protect Tate." And to himself: we have to watch over you, too.

"*Ohan.*" Yes. Iná climbed breathlessly into the pickup. "Your wife trouble enough."

It was almost dawn.

Iná got in beside Tate. "Both of you. Remember Turning Hawk Honor."

That didn't mean they would do nothing. Hokshicala was waiting, out of sight underground. But not for long. His mother was wrong. You could not bury crimes in the earth—Mother Earth will upturn them and expose them to the wind and sun.

CHAPTER 6
TATE

Iná's Midwife House, almost dawn

SHIVERING, TATE waited for Alex and Iná in the pickup. Poor Alex. She was merely too cold to rest, but he'd had to dig a grave and bury the dead baby in it. So wrong. She understood that he had to obey his mother in this—an elder—but what would happen someday when Alex would not follow Iná's commands? Maybe when she and Baby Turning Hawk moved back out in the country to Camp Crazy Horse. She missed being out in the country, the freshness of chokecherry blossoms, picking *cheyaka* for tea, the total darkness and silence at night. But she was too pregnant to haul water in cream cans from the creek and split firewood for the stove. Mabel, the camp cook, could handle the commodity rations to feed the hungry AIM work crew.

Now they would talk, figure things out, and then sleep the day through. She had said goodbye to Alex, who was supposed to go back to Camp Crazy Horse. But she knew, by his hand signals, that he would stay, come back to her, climb in the back bedroom window, and then they would decide what to do.

They'd have to protect Iná in spite of herself. And poor Iná, alone in her room with dark memories. That unquiet grave might haunt

Iná, turn her old overnight. It would haunt herself, too, like an old rerun horror movie. But she would be the strongest of them, because she'd stayed away from the criminal deed. She was Tate Two Hearts, ready to protect all four of them.

It was almost dawn when Alex drove them home. Tate handed Iná her cane, helped her up the steps to her room, and sat her down in her chair. Her mother-in-law looked so frail, so alone with her dark memories. She sat Iná in the chair beside her beading worktable and went into the kitchen, knowing what Iná needed: the horsemint tea fragrance whose filled the kitchen, and she brought a warm mug into the big bedroom.

The house was silent, full of sleeping people: midwives living in the basement, surrounded by dried herbs and quilt frames; their elder Grandma Agatha, in the small bedroom; niece Flossie and her toddler Buster asleep all day in the room next to the kitchen where Iná kept an eye on Flossie as well.

Iná sipped the tea in silence, but then struggled to get up from her chair. "We rest when we die. Now I get up, cook pancakes."

Tate stopped her and replied, "I'll do that, Iná."

Iná held up an eagle feather. "First make Alex take sweat, then you make prayer ties to protect our land and our Vision Cave."

Yes, she would help Alex purify the Vision Cave, renew the tobacco ties on the old altar, those over their cabin door, and those over his mother's kitchen door. She'd learned not to ask questions directly. "Tell me how it was, what you remember from long ago."

"End of Turning Hawks." Iná reached out to touch Tate's belly. "All depends on you. I live to see my grandson, he take care of me in old age. So Turning Hawk line never end."

Tate hadn't realized how much rested on Baby Two Heart in her belly. She'd share her baby with her mother-in-law. Iná was the Boss, but Tate had the Power, the miracle of women's power to give birth. It was women's magic, creating new life.

~~~

Iná had insisted that Alex go home to Camp Crazy Horse where he belonged, and purify the Turning Hawk Vision Cave. But Tate knew from his hand signal to her that he wouldn't obey his mother. She opened her bedroom window and leaned out, just far enough to see Alex's pickup hidden behind the shed next to the house. As he walked towards her, she ducked back inside and waited for him to climb in. As he hugged her, she asked, "Why doesn't Iná like me?"

"Oh, she likes you. She's proud of you." He brushed her hair back and kissed her.

"She doesn't like me, she only cares about our baby—her grandson." Tate turned away.

Alex laughed. "I can tell she likes you because she's hard on you to be perfect. If she didn't like you, she'd ignore you. If she yells at you, that means she cares about you. She was hard on me, too, so now I'm perfect."

She had to giggle at his big grin. Nearly naked, she locked the door. "Come to bed. Under the covers so Iná won't hear us."

While Alex took off his tee-shirt, she unbuckled his rodeo belt buckle. She'd been as proud by the "Junior Bareback Award" as if he'd returned from a war zone.

He crawled in beside her and cradled her belly holding their child. He leaned over and listened to the *tica-tica-tica* of his baby's heartbeat getting louder every day." All right, Tate Two Hearts," he teased. "Be as quiet as him inside you, making love." He kissed her ear.

She lay still in his arms. "Remember when we went to the clinic together and you were fascinated by the stethoscope when you heard the heartbeat?" He'd picked it up, wrinkling his brow, figuring how it worked, how it captured sounds. She wondered if he'd been making a stethoscope of rubber tubes and cedar for his patients, his visitors. Would he hear the heartbeat of animals? Wounded birds? Trees? He'd already told her Mother Earth's heartbeat lay beneath Paha Sapa, the sacred Black Hills, Center of the World.

He trembled in her arms, so she turned around in bed to rub the tension out of his back.

Mumbling into the pillows, he said, "When I was sad you would play and sing for me. Soon you can sing and play for our baby."

But she was a different Tate now. She'd given up the flashy difficult pieces she played alone out in the country, passionate crashing chords, but not here in town where she'd left the keyboard cover down so her piano wouldn't be pounded, mauled and wrecked. Instead she played quiet lullabies, the slow sections of a sonata, careful and even, legato and smooth. As Alex drifted off, she picked up her own abalone shell and a braid of sweetgrass. She lit one end of the braid, smudged her husband and lover, and sang a lullaby for him and Baby Two Heart. And fell asleep as well.

The afternoon sun woke her. The day half gone, and they were dealing with murder. Iná had said: say nothing. Yet they'd just buried a dead baby. It was wrong, but his mother had been so fierce and distraught, trying to hide some deep secret that would shame Turning Hawk Honor. It was time to decide what to do instead.

She kissed him awake, and sat up in bed. She knew the relatives called her Question Box, but she had to know things. She turned him around to face her. "Whose baby is it?"

"I don't know," he said. "But I do know Hokshicala was put in an old scorched Turning Hawk cradleboard."

"Iná says Turning Hawks wouldn't have used pink beads."

"Even though the red beads have faded to pink, it's our Vision Hill design."

"So she doesn't want to know." Tate cupped his face in her hands. "Because someone is out to get you, and maybe she knows who, and won't say." Hadn't he thought of it as a trap? "Did someone smother the baby for you to find, so you could be blamed for its death?"

"Probably just a threat. A warning." He brushed her hair away from his face.

"So black tobacco ties mean someone hates you." Was there a Lakota prayer for this?

"Yes, someone sent evil curses, bad medicine, but I already got rid of those ties."

"Weren't they around the baby's neck? And the smudged face? Does painting the face black mean death?"

"Wishing someone will die, yes. But we will pray against it."

"One more question. Who else knows about the Vision Cave?"

"Not many," he said. "Perhaps Até has returned and Iná recognized his cradleboard."

"Perhaps you wouldn't recognize him now," she said. Alex had no pictures of his father. At their Minneapolis wedding Alex had told her that Iná had burned all the photos of his father's rodeo wins. "Would your father know where his cemetery plot was? Who else would dig a tiny grave there, just waiting for us to find it?"

"He's been gone so long. I was only four, but I'm sure I'd know if it was him. Perhaps someone else is watching us, shadowing our family."

Tate turned over in bed. "Whatever Iná knows and won't tell us, it's still murder. We must take the dead baby to the cops."

"To the right cop, man to man, who'll keep it quiet," he said. "Tim New Holy comes on the night shift at the Eagle Nest substation. I left the spade in the pickup. Sneak me some food, let me sleep for an hour, and when it's dark I'll go rescue Hokshicala."

CHAPTER 7
ALEX

Tate's bedroom, after midnight

AS HIS wife fell asleep in his arms, he smiled at her determination. Tate Two Hearts. He was glad she'd found a second name. It made her strong, not whiney like so many pregnant women. But she didn't know, and he wasn't going to tell her that in Lakota, "two-hearts" was not a good thing. It meant not to be trusted, having both a good heart and a bad heart. And he'd heard that elsewhere in Indian country that there was a Two-Heart Society for *winktes*. Gays. If Tate was going to start a Lakota Two Heart Society for pregnant women, he'd have to warn her.

He remembered when Tate was first pregnant, she'd refused to use the old ways of the midwives, so he'd taken her instead to the Eagle Nest Indian Public Health to hear their baby's heartbeat. He'd been so fascinated by the stethoscope, examined it and wondered if he couldn't make one for himself for his own doctoring. Now she was so pregnant, he found it hard to fall asleep next to her with the baby inside kicking.

He dreamed of Hokshicala in the Spirit World, already smothered once, and smothered again while hidden in a grave underground.

Calling wordlessly for air. He must be rescued, given a proper burial, and his murderer found. Alex still had the spade.

He woke in the darkest of hours, dressed, and slid out the bedroom window and lifted the spade from the bed of his pickup hidden behind the storage shed. He didn't want his pickup noticed, so he walked silently in the night through the sleeping town to the Episcopal Cemetery. They'd agreed what Iná had done was wrong—covering up some ancient feud, some wrong or slight to Turning Hawk Honor.

Wind whished through the chokecherry branches. Overhead clouds covered the moon. Coyote howls faded in the distance. Beyond the fence he heard scrabbling in the brush, perhaps a badger or porcupine, digging to escape the town's dog pack. Or a drunk sleeping it off. He crept among the chokecherry bushes, but found no one. Only the Great Mystery was watching.

He fumbled with the latch at the iron gate, which creaked just as it had done the night before. In his haste, he hadn't brought oil to grease it. He waited until the moon came out again to see his path. Inside, white grave crosses stood like sentinels watching, watching, as if grave robbers might sneak in.

Alex found the small sod-covered grave outside the Turning Hawk plot, untouched by any digging animal. Until now. The grave was so fresh, he had no need for the sharp spade. He began to dig, removing the top grassy sod, laying it aside for later. As he sliced into the soft earth below, he sniffed. Had Hokshicala started to decay? No, the rottten smell came from behind. On guard, he swiveled around and swung the spade.

Thunk. He faced one of the ancient hulking veterans wearing a gigantic patched army parka and hairy black bear cap. Clarence, the local drunk. Big as a grizzly but harmless. He dropped the spade and thrust his hand out as if to a friend. *"Hau, kola."*

Clarence picked up the spade as if it were a toy shovel and swung it around. "Wha'chu doin' here? This is *my* cemetery. My job to guard it."

Alex stepped back and ducked. "Clarence, you *live* on the road to Interior Bar. You hitchhike back and forth, even in blizzards."

The giant hovered over Alex and the tiny open grave. "I may live on the road, but I crash in *my* bushes, way back outta sight." He nudged Alex's elbow. *"Chanli luha?"*

"Kolá,ohan." Yes, my friend. Alex offered him a packet of Bull Durham to roll his own.

Alex kicked at the loose dirt he'd unearthed. "So if this is *your* cemetery, it's your job to keep out grave robbers. Catch anybody?"

Clarence took his time rolling a smoke. "I run 'im off. Looked just like you, hawk nose."

"Young or old?"

"Middlin." He lit his cigarette and puffed.

"Wearing—"

"Army parka, like us? Nah, black leather. Boots, too. Not a cowboy."

His father Até had been broken by the rodeo. Maybe he'd changed to black city clothes.

Clarence hesitated. "Ooh, you *wichasha* holy men never carry a drop."

If only Alex had brought a jug, then Clarence would pass out in the bushes and forget. Then he'd talk up a story, but no one would believe him. He handed the giant his food packet.

Clarence walked into the bushes. *"Kola,* finish up, I never saw ya."

Kneeling, Alex scraped off the grass sod, flung off the dirt with his hands, and lifted the elk hide bundle into the moonlight. He brushed dirt off the hide and lifted the cradleboard's head cover so Hokshicala could see the moonlight. Alex sang in Lakota: "Released from this hole, we'll find your Turning Hawk mother or father so you can be properly buried and avenged."

Then headlights shone on the cemetery. Alex froze. Was someone else coming to sleep it off in the chokecherry bushes in the graveyard? Nah, Clarence would defend his hole-up. A ranch pickup drove into the back yard of the church, but turned toward the outhouse.

He relaxed. Only a proper drunk using the outhouse rather than pissing in the bushes. He waited until the pickup left, and his own heartbeat slowed down.

Carrying the black cradleboard in his arms, Alex slipped silently across town to Tate's bedroom window. The house was dark, which didn't mean that Iná wasn't watching. Only a tiny night light shone beside Tate's bed. She looked asleep, but as soon as he tapped the window, he saw her eyes open. Of course, why else would she leave the night light on? She was his accomplice in this rescue, moving soundlessly to raise the window. They had no need for words. Husband and wife, so easily they became of one mind.

Kneeling underneath the window, he unlaced the cradleboard, lifted Hokshicala out, now dressed in a white tablecloth, and wrapped him in the leather elk hide. Then he slid the black cradleboard up into Tate's hands. No need to show anyone else what might be his father's cradleboard. She would wash and purify it, fill in the missing beads, and hide it beneath her bed, safe until the mystery of Hokshicala would be solved.

She leaned at the window and whispered, "Alex, where's the spade?"

He looked down at his hands. He'd been so eager to escape

Clarence and rescue Hokshicala from the haunted cemetery.

Before he could answer, she reached her arms out and kissed him. "I'll get it before Iná sees it." She thrust a packet in his hands. "More frybread and money for gas on the road. Go!"

His mother, Hawk-eye Iná, saw everything. Almost everything. But so did Tate. Somehow his wife would make the spade disappear.

Now he had other worries. In the chill night air he carried Hokshicala through the fields to the Eagle Nest substation where Tim New Holy, a traditional sun dancer, was the cop on night shift duty.

The Eagle Nest substation was so new it smelled of fresh mortar and sawdust. The cement block building was surrounded by weeds and leftover lumber. Over the entrance hung a large floodlight left on both day and night. The huge garage door was open, revealing an Oglala Sioux Tribal black-and-white car and a steel cage with a cot inside for "protective custody—" Eagle Nest's version of the drunk tank. Behind sat a pool table and pop machine for bored cops.

Alex pulled onto the gravel in front and went in the office door. Behind a scarred desk and black phone with blinking red light and buttons on the side sat Tim New Holy, on night duty playing solitaire. Alex wondered why big men were so often peaceful at heart, while small scruffy men were so hotheaded and dangerous. His Law and Order Board had chosen Tim, Crazy Horse School's best linebacker, for their first man on their own Lakota police force. "Protect and Serve" was the motto, just as the ancient Kit Fox Society guarded Lakota camps on the plains.

Alex sat down on the donated church bench. "*Hau*, cuz. Cheating the cards again?"

Tim laughed. "More likely it's you cheating around, this time of night." Then he noticed the dirt-covered package in Alex's lap, and stopped. "You dig up something?"

Alex looked down at Hokshicala's bundle, which felt heavier by the minute. His heart felt heavier still, his tongue unable to find the words. But Tim was a traditional Indian who'd wait until the time was right for serious talk. "How's your wife?" Alex asked.

"She's fine." Tim grinned. "I got to see my son right away, birthed at home. Lena didn't go to Pine Ridge, heard rumors that the dead bodies haunt the hospital. They say the Morgue's in the basement, so ghosts float up at night to spook the nurses and patients."

Alex brushed dirt off his hands. "Got a smoke?"

Tim opened the desk, pulled out two cigarettes, lit them and handed one to Alex. "How far along is Tate?"

Alex blew out a circle of smoke. "Big as a curled-up porcupine. I stay out to the Camp."

"Heard your wife's in town, staying with your mother and the midwives. My wife saw Tate at the IPH clinic, going the modern way, probably sick of Iná's rubbing herbs and teas. But the midwives birthed you and me, and we're just fine."

How to explain Tate's change of mind? Alex puffed on his cigarette and began. "Iná told Tate about what it was like, being forced at Boarding School to go to the brand new White doctor, not an ignorant midwife. When Iná woke up from being drugged, she had to fight to get my birth cord. And after that, no more babies. Of course, being in town, Tate heard about babies dying at the Pine Ridge Hospital from the Moccasin Telegraph. Then last month she went with Flossie to a WARN meeting in Porcupine. Women of All Red Nations, she explained to me, and came back upset about some lawsuit."

"Hey, buddy," Tim said. "Let me warn you about WARN. Those feisty women dressed like men, swore like men, and fought like men in the trenches inside Wounded Knee Occupation in 1973. Now they're telling horror stories and demanding Women's Rights."

"Yes," Alex replied. His wife was probably one of them. When he finished smoking, he stubbed out the butt in a tin can on the floor and asked, "Any of those dying babies come from Eagle Nest?"

Tim replied, "No. We're a hundred miles away. Some say it's an epidemic like the 1918 flu. Rumors." Tim flipped through the police blotter pages until he found an entry. "Last week that Looking Horse girl said her baby turned blue and stopped breathing, so I did CPR, got it to cry and turn red in the face, back to normal. Heard it died on the way to the hospital."

Alex hesitated. "There's another one in my lap."

Tim blew out a stream of smoke, flipped his cigarette into the tin can, and pushed back his chair. "Someone came for medicine, but dumped it at the Camp?"

"In secret, for me to find."

Tim eyed the bundle, stared at Alex, and hesitated. "Uh-uh, *kolá*, yours?"

"Not mine." He wouldn't mention the Turning Hawk cradleboard in the Vision Cave, where Tim would fast before the Sundance, or the black tobacco tie necklace and painted face.

Tim brushed aside the Tribal card deck, reached in the desk drawer and pulled out the police roster. "Not a relative?"

"Unknown."

"So, you come on my shift, middle of the night, and want me to find this elk hide bundle left at the substation?"

"No, buddy, just keep it off the record." Tim would know about Pine Ridge's word-of-mouth Moccasin Telegraph. "So Camp Crazy Horse won't become a dumping ground." But what if someone had seen Iná before dawn at the Episcopal Cemetery? Or himself, at midnight, digging up the grave? "I'm not asking you to lie. When you get off duty, I'm asking you to drive me in your cruiser to the Pine Ridge Morgue."

Who could he ask about Iná in the olden days to explain her strange behavior now? "Something's wrong with Iná right now, off-center. You're from Corn Creek. Any idea what would make my mother go crazy? Any old rumors about her before I was born? Or my father?"

"Maybe Old Man Yellow Hawk might say something. Old-timers won't talk about the hardships, surviving Day School, or being sent away to Carlisle or Haskell Boarding School."

CHAPTER 8
TATE

Iná's House, early morning

AFTER ALEX handed her the old black cradleboard, Tate tucked it into one of their blankets, tied it securely, and slid the bundle far under the bed in case Iná came in to snoop. If Iná discovered the cradleboard, she'd have a fit and throw it out or burn it. But Alex thought it was his father's, a precious antique. Tate would clean it with cedar and sew new red beads into the Turning Hawk design.

If only she'd been laced in a cradleboard as a baby, safe and close, part of the family, not left in a crib alone in an empty room. So many cradleboards: Alex's cradleboard hanging like a trophy in Iná's room, this charred one under the bed, and the half-finished one Alex was making at Camp Crazy Horse for Baby Two Hearts. Would their own cradleboard be finished in time?

Another worry: how was she going to fetch the spade? Not just hide it, she realized, but Alex in his hurry, hadn't filled in the grave hole, hadn't put the mat of grass on top and smoothed it down so it looked undisturbed. Just in case Iná went up to the cemetery to check—and Iná would. The bedroom window was too high above

the half-basement to crawl through easily. Besides, the baby kicked
a lot now, making her big and clumsy.

Exhausted, she fell asleep. She dreamt that Iná was watching like
a mother hawk, ever since she'd caught Tate pouring the foul-tasting
tea—good for baby—down the sink. In the dream Tate gulped it
down, trying not to breathe. Iná might not like her, but she treated
her as a precious vessel carrying the tiny grandson waiting inside.
Iná was going to be surprised when a baby girl emerged, looking just
like Tate. Iná always pursed her lips in disapproval, shook her head
over every "mistake." Always reminding her that a medicine man's
wife didn't laugh too loud, didn't interrupt, didn't ask questions of
the elders.

Iná always got up before dawn to prepare food for all for the day.
Coffee, scrambled eggs and hash browns, pancakes with syrup. Next,
she'd knead frybread dough and set it aside to rise, to eat later with
beans and wild turnips simmering in the big pot. It was Iná's morning ritual, as prayer was Alex's morning ritual. Tate's was sleeping as
long as possible before having to pee.

As Tate dressed for the day, she struggled into a maternity blouse
that hung over her drawstring pants. She thought of stuffing the
pillow under her blouse just to give the old ladies a shock so they
could pester her about how big she was. Sure enough, as soon as she
came into the living room, Iná handed her a mug and said, "Drink!"

Iná stood at the stove in a floured apron. She turned and said to
Tate, who had gotten up from the clamor, "So you quit the Clinic.
Good. Stay away from that Pine Ridge Hospital and machines that
lift you upside-down and lock your legs in a steel frame. We know
what to do, walk you around, give you herbs, sing to you, hold you
when you're ready." Then she added in a tired raspy voice, "But now
you stay here, make beadwork for cradleboard, ready for baby."

"Yes, Iná."

The four old women—Mary, Martha, Mabel, Myrtle—living in the basement came upstairs to eat and gossip. They wore old-fashioned grey, brown, or black dresses and aprons, brown stockings rolled up to the knees, and black brogans. They braided their grey hair close to their heads. They folded bandages or brewed dark teas or sewed baby clothes.

With them came the fragrances from their work: dried herbs hung from the rafters—mint, chamomile, snakeroot—and baskets of dried chokecherries, wild plums, June and juniper berries. Most of them checked on Tate every day, since she'd committed the sin of going to the Eagle Nest Clinic once, and might have been given dangerous pills to swallow. As if their putrid herbal teas wouldn't kill her as well.

Then there was Grandma Agatha, the oldest, a distant relative, who lived above across from Tate. She spoke only Lakota, but so slowly and clearly that Tate had learned more words and phrases from her than from either Alex or Iná. These women were the "old maid aunties," widowed young without family or had lost a son or daughter to Relocation in big cities. "That's why, she thought, they like pregnant me and Buster the toddler. We're what they miss."

When Iná was widowed—so she said—she left the Turning Hawk land and moved into Eagle Nest to establish a "Midwife House," bought a black Ford station wagon named "Midwife Express" and began her traditional feud with the modern Indian Public Health clinic.

And how did Tate get stuck in the Midwife House until—it seemed forever? Alex had argued she was safer out in the country, away from drunks and fights in town. But Iná had won: safer in town with midwives. Iná had come to Camp Crazy Horse with her fancy cane and dragged Tate and her piano away from Alex and her horse—all because it wasn't "proper" for a pregnant woman to be around a camp full of young warriors, let alone ride horseback with them.

Tate went into the kitchen for a cup of coffee. Boiled coffee from the enamel pot—old-fashioned campfire style because the old ladies liked it that way, even though Iná had a modern drip coffee pot for visitors. Tate offered to help make frybread.

"Not ready," Iná said, shoving her out of the kitchen. "You finish sewing beaded bag for my grandson."

Other women in town came later on, drinking coffee and piecing star quilt tops, or bending over beadwork and quillwork, while a few descended into the basement to prepare poultices and salves. Old busybodies, Eagle Nest's grandmothers, coming together like a hive.

Tate sat on a couch opposite from Iná and picked up her beading. Iná stitched green and black beads onto a lizard bag for her grandson-to-come. Tate, sure her baby would be a girl, stitched brown and tan beads onto a turtle bag for her unborn daughter. It was a competition. Even though Tate was slower, she was determined to finish first. Under her breath she hummed a lullaby for her baby.

All of a sudden Buster, the restless two-year-old belonging to Cousin Flossie, stumbled out of the bedroom across from the kitchen, climbed onto the piano bench in the far corner of the living room, and looked around for Tate. "*Cha–cha*," he said. Meaning he wanted to play Chopsticks.

She laid aside her beadwork, scooted down next to him, and opened the piano lid. She'd given him lessons from her worn red Thompson's Basic Piano book. He didn't understand directions, but he had a musical ear, and he wasn't hopeless, like some of the other kids she'd taken on for lessons, just wired, day or night.

Buster loved to pound the lower keys, but today she sat him three octaves higher and pressed the mute pedal. She placed his small left fist on High C and his small right fist on an octave higher. "Which white block sounds the same?" She tapped his left fist and let him find the octave "block." She'd learned not to say *key* because Buster would cry. For him, *key* meant being locked in and left forever. "Yes," she sang, "C. Now where's the next C?"

Buster's fist pounded on middle C and sang "*wah*." The red nail-polish key that started every lesson. He clapped his hands together and bounced up and down on the piano bench.

Tate stood up and said, "Where's the next C, going down and down?"

Buster slid down the piano bench, punching every "white block" on the way until Tate's foot slipped off the mute pedal and he hit a crescendo exactly on low C: "Boom—Boom—Boom." He slid off the piano bench and laughed, happy with the echoes.

"Enough!" Iná cried, banging the floor with her diamond willow cane. "Either piano go or Buster go!" She stood up and stomped into the kitchen. "Before I Chopstick him."

Tate closed the keyboard lid. How unfair to Buster, who, amazingly, had near-perfect pitch. He looked cowed and ready to cry, as if he'd understood at least the tone of Iná's words, if not what they meant. She knew the threat was weak because Hawk-Eye Iná watched Flossie and Buster as much as Tate, and besides, *her* piano was the only one in Eagle Nest Housing and *her* lessons brought in money.

Tate picked Buster up and sang his favorite song, "Good night, Irene, good night." Which meant he got held and rocked to sleep. "Shhh," she said, and carried him into the bedroom across from the kitchen where he and his mother Flossie slept.

"Bang! Bang!"

Everyone looked for Buster, but this time someone was knocking at the kitchen door.

"Stop this racket," Iná yelled. Most of the midwives retired to the basement or left by the lower side door. Only Grandma Agatha and Tate remained in the room.

~~~

Iná opened the kitchen door slowly, as if reluctant for a stranger to interrupt the noise.

A tall Indian woman, taller than Iná, stood at the top of the steps. All Tate could see was her head: piercing black eyes, strong brows, and thick black hair parted in the middle, braided over her ears and disappearing into the brilliant colors of a Pendleton wool coat with a red-white-and-blue geometric design. She carried a black briefcase in one gloved hand.

The woman smiled. "I've been looking for 44 Eagle Nest Housing Loop, but the houses have no numbers. Is this where Tate Turning Hawk lives?"

Tate rushed toward the door, blocked by Iná, but she wiggled her way past to see who. Someone rich enough to own a Pendleton coat wanted to see her, Tate! She said, "That's me."

Iná switched to polite Boarding School English. "This is the Turning Hawk residence. What has my daughter-in-law done now? You come to fix the piano, the broken string? You are not from here, but her piano teacher, come all this way from Minneapolis?"

"Denver." The woman looked down at Tate and smiled. She had large perfectly white teeth. Then she looked at Iná. "I'm a lawyer. My specialty is Indian law. I drove a long way to find Eagle Nest Housing." She handed a business card to Iná.

Iná, who'd taken off her beading glasses to answer the door, handed it to Tate. "Read it."

Tate held the stiff white card with an Indian medicine wheel logo. She held it with both hands because they trembled. She took a breath and read, "It says, Belva Thundercloud, LLB. Denver Office of Indian Rights Association."

Iná responded, "An Indian lawyer? A lady Indian lawyer?"

Excited, Tate asked, "Dr. Belva Thundercloud, a Denver lawyer at last! I'd given up." The card was so smooth and thick. "May I keep the card?"

Iná grabbed the card. "I need to study this," she said, and carried it into the living room to find her beading glasses.

The woman stood on the threshold, statuesque, looked at Tate and smiled again. "I have more." She reached into a slot in her briefcase and handed Tate another card. "Before I enter, you understand, I'll wait for your mother-in-law."

Tate understood. This tall woman with a commanding presence had a sense of dignity and propriety. She would not enter unless invited by the matriarch.

From the living room, Iná emerged triumphant, wearing her glasses. She pushed Tate aside and shook Dr. Belva's gloved hand. "Please come in. First we will have coffee." She was still using her best Boarding School English. Tate's mother-in-law had realized that a Very Important Person had knocked at *her* door in Eagle Nest Housing. Not at the CAP Office, the IPH Clinic, the Crazy Horse School, or the Tribal Police Substation, but at her door, the house of midwives. Locals called it "The Gossip Hub," and it was as important as the Lakota warriors' AIM house directly across the housing circle, with its upside-down American flag painted on the outside wall. A Denver lawyer, even a woman from another tribe, would be a very useful prize.

"Yes. I'm here because of your daughter-in-law," Dr. Belva replied. "She wrote me a letter and asked me to come."

"A letter?" Iná asked. "This one here, barely out of school, wrote a letter to Denver?"

It must be the letter she'd written so long ago that she'd given up hope.

While Iná escorted Dr. Belva Thundercloud to the dining room table, Tate peeked out the kitchen door. A shiny black sedan was parked in the driveway. Who else besides the Tribal Chairman had a full-length Pendleton wool coat, drove a shiny black car that might be a Mercedes, and wore weird black leather gloves, the kind without fingers—for driving?

Iná, Auntie Agatha and Dr. Belva sat down at the dining table. Tate brought in plates and mugs of coffee, then silverware and their best linen napkins, and finally the warm puffy frybread and thick chokecherry jam. At last she sat down.

Dr. Belva took off her gloves and coat. Beneath it she wore a long red velvet skirt, a white long-sleeved blouse, a silver and turquoise squash blossom necklace, and a silver Concho belt and moccasins. From her stylish coat, gloves and briefcase, Tate had expected her to wear a business suit and heels like a career lawyer, a feminist here to gather evidence for a lawsuit. "Are you Chippewa?" She hoped not, since the Chippewa were traditional enemies of the Lakota.

"From my dress, I expected you to think I'm Navajo." Dr. Belva laughed. "Just as we the Diné don't call ourselves Navaho, you Lakota don't call yourself Sioux."

Iná replied, "Di-neh! Our woman lawyer is from a tribe in the Southwest. Now that you have arrived, you must stay here. I will introduce you to important people in town."

All of a sudden Iná's house was full, come to see the person who'd driven up the 44 Crazy Horse Drive in a fancy black car. A roomful of midwives and mothers sat on chairs, couches, or at the quilting frame, busy with crafts. And gossip, "about the lady lawyer, that big Navajo woman." When they all gathered together, Tate would introduce her as Diné.

Tate watched as Dr. Belva stood and shook each woman's hand as she passed around the circle, then sat back down at the dining table.

A feast appeared from the kitchen, some from others' houses, enough for all: beef and wild turnip stew, puffy frybread and flat *kabuk* bread, ending with *wojapi*, a ground chokecherry pudding, and more coffee. Iná brought in food and more food. "Pass the plates and food around."

Tate got it. The women seated on couches and around the quilt frame, crowded and as uncomfortable as they were, would stay to hear the Denver Indian lady lawyer.

Tate held her breath as Dr. Belva handed Tate's letter across the dining table to Iná.

Iná adjusted her glasses and read loud and clearly, probably to show that she hadn't forgotten her Indian Boarding School's elocutions lessons. "To Whom It May Concern?" She skimmed the letter. "Mrs. Alex Turning Hawk? Does my son know about this?"

Tate had almost forgotten about the WARN meeting in Porcupine. "Not yet."

Iná looked at Tate. "So you sent this letter to a Denver lawyer to collect papers for our lawsuit? You are a smart girl, after all." Iná's eyes sparkled as she turned to Dr. Belva. "You've come here to help us win our Black Hills back! My son Alex, along with Old Treaty Council and AIM warriors, marched to D. C. so the President of the United States must honor 1868 Fort Laramie Treaty and Great Sioux Nation lawsuit."

Tate was surprised at Iná's knowledge. Alex hadn't told her that he'd been at the Trail of Broken Treaties, only that he'd been at the AIM trials after Wounded Knee Occupation in 1973.

Iná said to Dr. Belva, "Explain to us why nothing has been happening with our Black Hills Claim." She passed Tate's letter to Auntie Agatha, who held it, but didn't read it, and then passed it back to Iná.

Dr. Belva remained silent, her slender hands folded in her lap. Tate shifted in her chair. Auntie Agatha nodded, either in agreed-upon silence, or else half-asleep.

Iná read more of the letter. "What is this thing, WARN? Warn us against what?"

Tate said, "It means, Women of All Red Nations."

"We have heard of those upstart half-breeds in Porcupine—" Iná paused. "Was that when Flossie sneaked off with you in her mother's car to look for boys?"

Iná probably thought it was Flossie's idea, since Flossie knew all the Eagle Nest boys.

Iná continued, "Only Old Treaty Descendants go to Washington for lawsuits. What do these Red Women want with our Lakota lawsuit? We do not need"—she hesitated—"af-fa-day-vits? But we will listen to your story."

Tate had forgotten that her letter had asked about collecting signed papers for evidence.

Iná went into her bedroom, returned with her diamond willow cane, and stood beside Dr. Belva. She thumped the floor, calling a house meeting to order. *"Mashke."* Women friends. "An Indian lawyer, Belva Thundercloud, has come all the way from Navajo land to Eagle Nest to help us with lawsuits. Now listen." She turned to Dr. Belva. *"Pilamaya.* Thank you."

As Dr. Belva stood, taller than Iná, she took command of the room, smiling at each woman sitting on couches or folding chairs. "Evidence," she called out. "Just like your Old Treaty Descendants took the original documents to D.C. to prove their claim, we women need evidence, too, to prove our claim in Washington, D.C., as well."

Iná asked, "Has the claim about tribal land theft, lease money withheld, allotments, been taken over by the Bureau of Indian Affairs?"

Dr. Belva paused.

Tate, still seated at the table, flinched. A great misunderstanding was coming. If only she'd told a little bit about the WARN meeting, and the lawsuit—which she hadn't dared, because Iná wouldn't have listened anyway.

"No," said Dr. Belva. "Sterilization. It's a case of forced genocide. We're bringing suit against the Bureau of Indian Public Health. Thirty years ago, Indian women of child-bearing age, particularly on Pine Ridge Reservation, were sterilized without their knowledge or permission. We're collecting data, seeking out plaintiffs as witnesses for the case."

Sterilization. What was the Lakota word for it? Or was there one? Tate waited to hear the midwives' reactions: "*Iteshni?*" Which meant, "Oh, my, really?" But no one spoke. Instead, women bent over their beadwork, four sitting at the quilt frame hanging from the ceiling, sewing intently, looking at their stitches but with ears alert to catch every nuance. Tate realized that the women might all be sterile. Auntie Agatha wouldn't have understood, but the others had.

To fill the gap, Iná pointed at Tate and flicked her wrist toward the kitchen, meaning: bring in more food. Iná added, "*Inachni!*" which meant, "hurry up."

Tate understood. The women seated on couches and around the quilt frame, ready to leave with a dozen excuses, would have to stay. It was rude to refuse food, and if someone did, she'd not be welcome again. Iná was not letting anyone escape from Dr. Belva's terrible request. Otherwise Iná could lose face. And perhaps lose her Very Important Person as well.

Tate ran into the kitchen and carried out the pot of remaining stew, frybread and jam. Then she refilled their mugs with warm coffee.

A few middle-aged women responded with "hnnn." Old women didn't talk about such things. Tate knew that some had only one child, some none—shameful for a Lakota woman.

Dr. Belva looked expectantly around the room. "We're looking especially for women who were of child-bearing age in the 50s and 60s, women who went to the Pine Ridge Hospital to have their babies the new modern way, women who were anesthetized for painless childbirth, and had their tubes tied or uteruses removed at the same time as giving birth."

Sterilizaton. The grandmas talked in Lakota now, not the usual slow cadences, but the fast gossipy style, emphatic phrases Tate couldn't understand. They wouldn't talk about such things in English. Lakota pride! None of them would admit to being infertile, none would share intimate physical details, none would admit that they'd been talked into going White Way to have their babies at the new very sanitary hospital in Pine Ridge instead of going to the heathen midwives of the old traditional ways to miscarry or lose their baby at childbirth.

Dr. Belva asked Tate to translate what they were saying. She didn't know the words, but she knew what was going on. There was Iná, painfully aware of her inability to produce another child after Alex. Once it was honorable to have many children, spaced every three to four years, through natural herbs that prevented pregnancy until the mother was finished nursing. No wonder Iná and the others doted so much on their *takojas,* grandchildren.

"Sorry, Dr. Belva," Tate said, "they're talking in the old language, a Lakota that I don't understand. But it means they do understand what you're saying."

"Good," Dr. Belva stood up and walked around the room. "Ladies, we've found records buried in the Smithsonian archives basement documenting the procedures. The doctors were proud of their work! But the records are by Tribal number, not individual names. So we're looking for women in this age range who have had only one child."

More silence. Auntie Agatha had the good sense to fall asleep in her chair.

Iná asked Dr. Belva about her journey from Denver.

Some women folded up their quillwork or beadwork, while others raised the quilt frame overhead to the hooks in the ceiling, out of the way.

"Please come back another day," Dr. Belva said. The townswomen nodded, yes, shook hands, and thanked her: "*Pilamaya.*" Then the midwives descended to the basement, while others from town left by the side door.

CHAPTER 9
ALEX

Pine Ridge Hospital Morgue, late morning

ALEX WOKE up two hours and a hundred miles later. He'd been dreaming that he'd finished the wooden cradleboard for Tate and his baby. He looked at his hands, still holding Hokshicala in his lap, bundled only in a tablecloth and elk hide. *Unshica.* Poor one. He asked Tim New Holy, "Are we at the Pine Ridge Morgue yet?"

"You been snoring for miles, bro." Tim circled the IPH hospital and parked in the back, near the basement entrance to the Morgue. From the dashboard he pocketed a bunch of braided sweetgrass and said, "Get ready for the Underworld."

Beside the steps sat a battered black Harley, locked with a steel chain. Fancy powerful cycles like that were rare on the Res, too easily lifted and sold in Rapid City or Omaha. Macho dudes on the Res drove heavy high-center balloon-tire rigs with deer lights—until the Repo Man caught up. This bike had a decal of a spider on the chassis.

Alex hid Hokshicala under his jacket, got out, and stopped in front of the cement steps leading deep underground. He'd never been in the Morgue. Medicine men didn't go there. But he'd already dug up a dead baby that belonged here to be identified and claimed. As he followed Tim down the steps to an underworld where the dead were kept isolated from the living patients far above, he agreed with the Res gossips who felt this was wrong.

But when Tim opened the steel door, Alex followed. Inside was cold, not as cold as a food locker, but cold enough to heighten the smells of formaldehyde, dead bodies, alcohol, cigarettes, and metal. Metal walls, trays, tables, overhead lights, tools: *maza,* dug from deep in the earth, the opposite of *chan,* wood, from which everything sacred was made. Hair at the back of his neck rose. In the big room he sensed a sharp disquieting energy, not repose. Empty.

"Creepy, *ennit?*" Tim said from ahead of Alex. "Part of my job, dealing with car wrecks, old gents' bodies, suicides. As a cop I had to get used to it."

A light glowed in the back hallway. Tim called out, "Anybody here?" When he heard no answer, he strode past the metal tables, some covered with draped cloth, and knocked on another door. A dark figure emerged, shadowed by the light behind, wearing a gray plastic apron over green hospital garb. He looked Chicano, his black hair in a ponytail. His tattooed hands and scarred face marked him as a street fighter. The Harley above must be his. Indian Public Health had to hire non-Indians who didn't mind touching dead bodies, who didn't believe in ghosts. Though with his dark skin and big nose, he might try to pass as Indian.

Still ignoring Alex, the man sauntered over to Tim, scuffing the cement floor. Beneath his apron and scrubs he wore black biker boots decorated with chains at the ankles. He shook Tim's hand and in a bantering familiar way asked, "Hey, New Holy, wha'chu brought me? Another dead baby?"

Alex noticed his thick Spanish accent, and backed into the shadows so he could watch unseen what this stranger was like. The guy had called Tim by name, not as a cop, but as a rookie whom he knew. How could it be that they were buddies, acting like old friends? Had Tim brought other bodies here from Eagle Nest?

Alex picked up the clipboard roster that had been drawn up for the day and flipped the page back several months. "Do you have these death stats for several years back?"

Ignoring Alex, the man walked over to Tim. "Easy. Boring. Lots of infants since I started here. Cause of death varies, but mostly SIDS, or birth defects, or 'failure to thrive.' That's what the doctors write when they don't know."

"What happens to a dead baby?" Alex asked.

At last the guy looked at him and shrugged. "Dunno. I just put them in the Morgue's cold room until some Tribal official takes 'em away."

A cold reaction. Were the bodies taken off-Res to be cut open and autopsied, part of an Indian Public Health study? Or were they cremated or buried with the unknown graves in the Pine Ridge Cemetery. "Will there be an autopsy?" Alex asked. He didn't want Hokshicala to be cut up into pieces and destroyed, but to be buried whole.

Alex's question made the guy stare, as if he were throwing knives from his eyes. "Hey, Tim, who is your ride-along?"

Tim looked up from the list. "My buddy's got a baby death."

Alex kept his gaze steady. "We need more info about SIDS and unknown diseases. How many desertions, negligence versus murders, and trials versus convictions."

"They don't let me see that kind of information. The closest I get is hospital charts."

Alex moved in closer. "As a med student you must have noticed something."

The guy smiled slightly and faced Alex. "I'm Zack Espada, the new Morgue attendant. How can I help *you*?" His voice sounded flat and polite, but with a heavy sing-song accent.

A metal stretcher lay between them. Instead of responding with his name, Alex eased the bundle from under his jacket onto the white sheet, reluctant to release Hokshicala to this uncaring man. He'd carried a naked baby close to his heart a hundred miles from the Vision Cave to the World of the Underground, and he wasn't about to be polite and give his name.

Zack unwrapped the elk hide and the white tablecloth to reveal a naked baby boy. "You found him alive?" Quickly he draped a sheet over the dead baby.

Alex was surprised at Zack's reactions: shock, revulsion, then delicacy as he'd rewrapped the dead baby and walked away from the gurney as if nothing had happened. Maybe this Chicano with his black boots and black Harley fit the job. Alex answered, "Not alive, but not dead long."

"Why didn't you bring him in a box?" Zack sounded indignant.

As if Eagle Nest had small coffins lying around. "We use elk hide, rare these days," Alex explained, "to honor the dead."

"Well, I've seen 'em all." Zack had shifted to nonchalance. "Hey, New Holy, you didn't warn me this guy brought another one." Zack waved his arms as if to wave away dead babies. "Must be a lotta sickness on your end of the Res."

Tim walked over to Alex and said in Lakota, "Buckle up, *kola*." Which meant in rodeo slang: hang on. Then he handed Zack an Eagle Nest log book and pen. "Need you to sign off."

Zack scribbled, shrugged, and walked back to a desk at the rear. "Now you need to sign off on my ledger. Both of you. You can't just leave a corpse without a case number. I have to fill in the 'who-what-when-where' for the record."

Tim filled in the form while Alex looked on without correcting him:

Who: Unknown person
What: left a elk hide bundle
When: 4:10 a.m.
Where: at the door of Eagle Nest Substation.

Testimony: Night duty police checked with flashlight around
Substation for traces of persons unknown, then returned to
examine bundle, and discovered a dead baby, sex, boy. No
baby bracelet. No name. Arrival Pine Ridge Morgue, 10:37
a.m. Signed, Tim New Holy, Eagle Nest Tribal Police.

Alex signed after Tim. He was tempted to add the tag some med-
icine men used, M.M.—Medicine Man—mocking Catholic priests'
SJ or doctors' MD, but instead wrote simply Turning Hawk, Alex.
That name was powerful enough.

Zack looked at the signature. He seemed impressed. "So, Alex
Turning Hawk, you're not a cop, not an ambulance driver, not an
EMT. Who are you to sign?" Zack waved the ledger at Tim. "Why'd
you bring him along?"

Tim looked away. Finally he said, "Spooky ride. I needed his
prayers all the way."

Alex replied, "*Ohan, wichasha wakan,*" Yes, I am a medicine man.

Zack looked surprised. "If he really is a medicine man, he can
only sign as a witness."

As Zack reached out to claim the Tribal Registry of the Dead, a
chain popped loose from his pants, a medal like the St. Christopher
medals they gave out at Holy Rosary Mission. Maybe he carried a
rosary in his pocket, like the tobacco ties in his own.

"So you are a Catholic undertaker," Alex said.

Zack shook his head vehemently. "My religion is none of your
business, and wha'chu got against the Catholic Church? I was born
into Catholic Services."

"No offense." Alex backed off. "In the olden days, many of our elders were forced to be Catholic, but now we healers work together to keep the People strong."

"Besides, I am not an undertaker." Zack's voice grew louder and louder. "I am not a mortician. I'm not the embalmer or a forensic technician. I just do my job as an attendant."

How strange to find a man who felt more at home in a cold basement dungeon without windows, filled with acrid antiseptic odors and dead bodies. Alex asked, "How do you stand it?"

Zack replied, "Where I come from, every night dead bodies lie in the streets from shootouts. Here and alive, the dead don't shoot. This Internship gets me into Med School."

Zack must have filled in all the IPH, BIA and OST forms, to sign a Tribal contract. Alex asked, "But how'd you get the job?"

Zack laughed. "No one here would touch dead bodies. Me, I don't care. I don't know them, and *ha-ha* they can't harm me. Easy job, good pay, free housing, lots of Pine Ridge putas."

Alex guessed what 'putas' meant. Zack was getting even with them for using Lakota. "Well, I guess it's worth it to you."

"Oh, yes!" Zack stared at him as if from far away. "Some are born to birth, some are born to death. And you?"

Profound words from a young intern made Alex think. Unlike Zack, he'd been born to walk in both worlds, the living and the dead, similar to his mother the midwife and undertaker.

"Caramba!" Zack's taunting voice returned. "I've been looking for a certain kind of curandero. Is it true that you can cure love sickness? El sueño? They say you work miracles."

Miracles like Jesus-of-Nazareth miracles. "Only the Great Mystery works miracles," Alex replied. "People come to me for healing. I pray to the Great Mystery and help them heal themselves. But this—is it a new disease, or just 'failure to thrive?' I need to find a cure."

"If you work here long enough, you learn there is no cure for death. Que será, será."

Alex had heard the phrase, "What will be, will be." Obviously Zack was a fatalist.

Zack waved his hands, as if he wanted them leave.

Alex had memorized the Morgue attendant's name, although he didn't expect to meet him nor enter his Underworld again. He was handing Hokshicala's spirit over to another who seemed so hard-hearted. Alex could not stop himself. "This baby was once alive and needed a name. Hokshicala is an affectionate name in Lakota, which means in English, Little Baby Boy."

"What? He's yours? Tim said he was deserted at the Eagle Nest Substation."

"Mine hasn't been born yet. But this baby must enter the Spirit World with a name."

Zack whipped out his knife, cut the tag loose, and tied another tag onto the tiny foot. "No room to spell that "Hoke-something-or-other."

Alex could not stop himself. He grabbed the black pen from Zack and marked the tag:

Turning Hawk. "There! Turning Hawk!"

The name echoed around the Morgue. Maybe the baby *was* a Turning Hawk relative.

Tim grabbed Alex by the shoulders. "*Kolá*, what are you doing?"

Zack, still holding his knife, turned pale. Dead black eyes bored into Alex's.

Alex stared back. "I take responsibility. For praying for Hokshicala into the Spirit World. I am a medicine man and give this poor dead baby a better name than "Unknown."

Also responsibility to find who'd smothered Hokshicala, put him in an old cradleboard, and hid him in the Vision Cave. He hated to think that person might have been his father.

~~~

Hokshicala was out of Alex's hands now, lost to the cold depth of the Morgue. Other dead babies had been left there as well, tagged as 'failure to thrive' or *'no known cause.'* The new Morgue attendant hadn't recognized the symptoms that Iná had seen. He'd find out if there were other Turning Hawks on the Res, or at Eagle Butte or Rosebud.

Outside the Morgue, Tim strode over to the cruiser and opened the back door. "You crazy? Just broadcasting all over the Res that you turned in a dead baby Turning Hawk. So proud of your family name. Wait until your mother hears, let alone your wife. Put out your hands."

Alex, still thinking of searching for Até, obeyed.

Immediately Tim handcuffed Alex. "Get in the cruiser and duck down." He pushed Alex into the back seat and slammed the door, which locked automatically. "I gotta take my report to the Pine Ridge Station. Can't lose my job by having a passenger in a Tribal cruiser," Tim yelled as he climbed the Station steps and went inside. "Not unless he's been arrested and ready to be transported."

Alex had been handcuffed and arrested before, but not by a friend. He wasn't sure if Tim was really angry, just acting, or scared of his Pine Ridge lieutenant. The harsh metal cut into his skin, but he reached forward to grab his small fasting pipe on the dashboard. Lying back down on the back seat, he managed to slide it safely into his parka pocket.

At last Tim stumbled down the Station steps and climbed into the cruiser. He turned around and with a wicked smile, said, "Ain't you the lucky one. Emergency call from Eagle Nest substation says: 'Wanted immediately, Alex Turning Hawk at Camp Crazy Horse, matter of life or death.' So I get to drive this criminal a hundred miles an hour home and uncuff him in front of all his warriors."

Alex didn't care. As a new medicine man, his first visitor had arrived. Excited, he hoped it was his father. He explained to Tim, "Whoever comes to us for help, we don't call them sick 'patients' or business 'clients', but 'visitors' because often they are caught between two worlds."

CHAPTER 10
TATE

Ina's House late morning

WHAT SHATTERING news Dr. Belva had brought. To think that instead of being shamefully infertile, they and their husbands were not at fault. That it had been a plot against the Indian Nations, that it wasn't paranoia to experience prejudice, a threat to the Tribe's continuity. Tate imagined all the leaders and mothers not born. No wonder such poverty, alcoholism and despair.

It didn't take long for Iná to recover. Of course she'd capture Dr. Belva and brag about hosting an Important Government lawyer, the better to keep informed on the progress of Dr. Belva's trip, and to find out which Lakota women had told what secrets from way back in the Boarding School days.

Iná sat down across from Dr. Belva and announced, "You will stay here."

Dr. Belva swept her eyes around the room full of empty couches and chairs. "Thank you, but I'll look for a motel later."

Siding with Iná, for a change, Tate jumped in. "There's no motels on the Res, and if you stay thirty miles away in Kadoka or Hot

Springs, you'll offend Lakota hospitality. The AIM house in town is full up with young men. My mother-in-law Iná—you can call her Agnes—wants you to stay here. We're in the center of things, a gathering place for quilters and bead workers, the generation of elders you're seeking. Besides, the best way to interview Iná is here."

"We will prepare a feast in honor of our new guest," Iná announced to the empty room, "Cook food, sew blankets, shawl, big meeting at the CAP Office." Then she disappeared into the bedroom off the kitchen, the one which Flossie and Buster occupied.

Dr. Belva looked around. Tate guessed she was looking for the bathroom, and showed her the way. Fortunately, all Eagle Nest houses had indoor plumbing, unlike the Episcopal Church with its wooden outhouse. Then Tate went into the kitchen, piled unwashed dishes and mugs, and filled the sink with soapy water.

Iná started ranting in Lakota in an aggrieved tone. In the kitchen, Tate caught the gist: "I take my niece in, no one wants Buster, from your mother's drunk house, you a bad influence on Tate, took your mother's car, drove to Porcupine to meet boys, and both of you pregnant! From the mouth of mother of Tim New Holy, I hear it."

Flossie answering in Lakota: "No one hits my Buster. No matter what kind of sticks."

Tate had seen it coming when Iná threatened to 'chopstick Buster.' Iná had been waiting for an excuse, and the perfect excuse appeared with the arrival of a VIP woman lawyer.

When Dr. Belva returned from the bathroom, bewildered by the Lakota-language dialogue, she asked Tate, "What is happening now?"

Tate explained, "All Flossie and I did was go to join WARN to do something for Indian Rights and learn about the lawsuit. That's when I wrote you the letter that Iná has now. So even though she's mad at us, really she's tired of Flossie and Buster, her niece and grand-nephew."

Dr. Belva hesitated. "Oh. I could never—"

Tate interrupted, "It would be wise to stay here. Safest. You've met Iná. She's the head Traditional person in town. She knows everybody and everything going on. People are scared of her. Some call her a witch. Even my husband is scared of her. Me, too, sometimes."

Iná stomped out of Flossie's room, yelling "*Inach-ni, inach-ni!*" Which meant: hurry-up. She threw Buster's toy cars scattered around the living room into a satchel, opened the kitchen door, and threw it outside. Then she bustled back into the bedroom.

Flossie slammed the door shut after her.

Belva said hesitantly, "Perhaps—"

Tate interrupted. "Once Iná makes up her mind, that's it. You don't cross her. I've learned the hard way. She calls me 'Question Box' all the time, but I just keep my mouth shut. One good thing about her, though—she keeps my foster mother away. If that woman ever tried to take me 'home' again, Iná would slam the door in her face. She'd never lose me—and her grandson inside me. But as soon as I have this baby, we're—my husband and me—we'll move back to Camp Crazy Horse on Turning Hawk land and begin our lives together."

Dr. Belva laughed and said, "At home it's the same. We Diné women are boss of our hogans, our flocks of sheep, our wool, and our looms on which we weave our rugs."

"So you understand that you have to stay here? Once you stepped inside, you were caught. Just like me. When she learned I was pregnant, she came and took my piano into her house in town, knowing that I'd go with it."

She reached for Dr. Belva's hand. "Come into my bedroom away from the ruckus. I'll show you an ancient cradleboard I'm repairing."

Iná, breathless, sat down at the table, drank the rest of her coffee, and spoke to Dr. Belva. "Welcome. Now your room is ready for you to stay here." Iná, handing Dr. Belva a fresh towel and wash cloth, ushered Dr. Belva into the neatly-made bed and newly-cleared room. The spare bedroom off the kitchen had been washed and swept. Lakota posters hung on the walls, and an eight-pointed star quilt covered the bed.

Gone were Flossie's and Buster's clothes, toys, and the small TV—to her mother's house across the street. Tate was glad that at least Iná hadn't found Flossie's stash of dope. She'd miss Buster, but perhaps she'd sneak him in to practice while Iná was away.

Iná said, "Since you stay here for a visit, my daughter-in-law will show you the town of Eagle Nest. So you can find your way around. Later on, we will kill a beef in your honor, invite our tribal headman and our *eyapaha*, our town-crier, so that we can help you in your work."

Tate sighed. Iná had taken over Dr. Belva. But not for long. Every day she'd drive Dr. Belva around the Res until they had enough affidavits collected before any trial began. She'd learn how the Law worked so she could become a lawyer herself some day.

She helped Dr. Belva unlock the shiny black rental Mercedes with its black leather seats, and leather stick shift. What fun it would be to drive around the Res. Dr. Belva traveled light: coat, gloves, purse, briefcase, typewriter, tape recorder, and a small suitcase. She hauled Dr. Belva's suitcase up the concrete steps and into the VIP guest's new room.

A few minutes later, Dr. Belva emerged. The three of them sat down at the dining room table with leftovers for supper. "Tate," she asked, "What was it you couldn't translate?"

What could Tate say? "I think 'sterilization' was the key that started them talking in Lakota. That English word scared them."

For once, Iná covered for her, knowing Tate knew little of the old Lakota language. Iná explained to Dr. Belva that it had been too much for the old ladies to take in all at once because they hadn't been sent to Boarding School to learn proper English from the nuns, as she had.

Dr. Belva must have been raised in the city. Hadn't she realized these old Lakota ladies were shrewd, canny, and even vicious, full of stubborn pride and skilled at evasion? They'd bested BIA land clerks for years to get lease monies owed. Dr. Belva had never seen them stamp down a full house card at Bingo, trumping the rest of the senior citizens with a loud voice. Or screaming a *li-li-li* victory cry at a memorial dinner or for a returning veteran. Slashing their legs in mourn for a lost relative. They knew what sterilization was, and weren't about to talk about it.

Dr. Belva had started out too directly, expecting these old women to reveal private, personal matters. So they'd managed to remain dumb, uttering silly phrases like 'No speak English.' Tate had heard them, but she managed not to giggle and ruin their cover.

Iná stepped in to divert Dr. Belva. "But I will bring the modern ones to you, who brag that their kids speak only English."

That wouldn't work for Dr. Belva's getting affidavits. The younger Eagle Nest mothers with half a dozen kids would talk about Pampers, bottle formulas and cribs. And others would talk about the traditions of gathering moss, making cradleboards and breast feeding. Iná had boxed herself into a corner.

But Tate could save face for Iná. She'd take Dr. Belva to the College trailers where more modern women were, those who worked and studied to be nurses and teachers' aides. Even if older women used Lakota or broken English, they would speak slowly, and she could translate, one on one. "I can be your *ieska*, your translator."

Dr. Belva smiled. "Can you type? I'll need a navigator and secretary as well."

"Oh, yes," Tate said. "I took typing in high school." Dr. Belva was a *toka*, an outsider, an urban Apple—red on the outside and white on the inside—and she didn't realize that Tate was red on the outside, but still white inside. But she'd get Alex to help open the door to some of the AIM grandmas, bold activists who might give up privacy for courtroom drama: Moves Camp at Ring Thunder, Red Eyes in Manderson, others who were inside the Wounded Knee '73 Occupation. Fullbloods fluent in both Lakota and English.

"She's too pregnant," Iná replied. The fact that she didn't mention that Tate knew very little Lakota meant that Iná was weakening in her objections to Tate riding along.

She wasn't too pregnant. She was Tate Two Hearts, stronger than Iná. Younger. Smarter. "And I can drive," she added. "I know the Res roads. And I'm the only one around with a valid S.D. driver's license! Besides, no man can drive Dr. Belva around without a scandal. Everyone would shun her, not even let her in the door, and some old widow might even spit on her."

Dr. Belva looked at Tate's belly and smiled. "Good. I understand you know the reservation and can direct me around to visit some of the remote elders. But I'll drive."

Oh. Maybe she'd change her mind when she got stuck on one of the potholed roads. Tate turned to Iná. "Hear that? I could deliver beadwork or herbs to Auntie Violet." Maybe she'd see Alex on the way, a slight detour, she'd explain. Alex would laugh at her being an *ieska*, an interpreter—the same word for his role as *ieska* now, interpreter with the Spirit People in ceremony. Still, she could interpret what people might be thinking, feeling or doing. "I'll help you find witnesses. This is an important case for justice delayed."

Question Box on the move. She'd ask the questions. She could be young and silly: "How come no kids?" Too direct. "Were you ever married?" "Where did you used to live?" The older women would pity her, and give her vague answers. The modern women with no shame would ask for money to sign. They'd get enough affidavits to win the lawsuit.

After dark the Housing Circle streetlights flickered and went out. Again. It was Iná's routine to turn out the house lights as well: end the day and go to bed. A few minutes later Tate heard a soft knocking on her door. Dr. Belva. She'd had a long flight from Denver to Rapid City, and a long drive on Reservation roads. Maybe she couldn't sleep. "Come in, please, and have some Indian tea."

Dr. Belva sat down at the bottom of Tate's bed. "Is there a phone in the house?" she asked. "I need to call and let my office know I've arrived safely."

No house in town had a phone; everyone counted on the Moccasin Telegraph. The CAP Office, Clinic, and School were closed. "You could try the Substation—or the Mormons."

Dr. Belva hesitated. "Usually two of us travel to collect evidence for the lawsuit, but it's been hectic at the office. I expected to drive, but the Director said it took too long, meaning he didn't want me alone on the road at night. So I flew and rented a car in Rapid City. When I got to the rental booth, another man stood behind me. He stood too close, as if he were looking over my shoulder at my itinerary. He might try to follow me, so I drove off before he came outside."

Tate reached out to touch Dr. Belva's hand. "That's why you must stay here: we're protected." Tate pointed to Alex's small red string of tobacco ties over the bedroom door.

"I recognize it," Dr. Belva replied. "It's similar to one over the door at our law office in Denver." She touched her silver necklace and added, "But my Navaho protection goes with me."

Tate had already admired the silver squash blossom necklace. Now, as it gleamed in the empty room, she felt its power—not just jewelry, but medicine in every blossom. How amazing that different tribes shaped spiritual prayers to look like innocuous works of art.

Dr. Belva shrugged. "It's been a long day. Tomorrow will be fine."

CHAPTER 11
ALEX

Camp Crazy Horse, early afternoon

AT THE big gate to Camp Crazy Horse with its car hood sign—
"NO ALCOHOL NO DOPE NO GUNS—Tim hauled Alex out of
the cruiser and un-cuffed him. "OK, Bro, I gotta check in at the
Substation and write my report. You got more on your hands than I
do, someone dying's worse than Moccasin Telegraph gossip. Better
stay home, though, and avoid town."

Stiff from being handcuffed, Alex walked down toward the
Sundance grounds below. Several of the camp warriors, Ben, Chaské,
Old Louie, and Baxter, stood around the fire pit, smoking and watching the big stones glow red-hot. Nearby the tarp-covered sweat lodge
was open. Usually they started a sweat lodge fire in the evening, not
mid-afternoon. "Thanks for getting the sweat ready for my life-or-
death *visitor*." He looked around. "Where's Smokey?"

Silence. Finally, Old Louie waved a hand toward the sweat lodge.

Alex walked over and peered in. Smokey, his second-in-com-
mand, a bronc-riding cowboy known for his grey-green eyes and
wide smile, crouched in the south side. Smokey wasn't smiling. He

was cringing, completely clothed, his boots scraping the packed earth.

"Hiding in the sweat lodge?" Alex asked, annoyed. "Where's the dying visitor?"

Smokey crawled out and grabbed Alex by the shoulders. "My savior! Damn it, Alex, whenever you're home, it's peaceful. But every time you leave camp, trouble arrives and I have to deal with it. Camp Crazy Horse is supposed to be a Sanctuary, but I get no peace at all."

Alex punched him back. "Well, certainly *you* aren't dying. What's going on?"

Smokey shuffled his feet. "Told her to come back later, but she said she'd wait."

Alex couldn't imagine Smokey scared of an old Indian lady. He didn't recognize the dilapidated car parked in front of his cabin. "What's so life-and-death, then?" he asked.

Behind him the warriors around the fire pit snickered.

Heat rose in his body, toe to head. All the way home he'd worried that whoever had left Hokshicala in the Vision Cave might have planted black tobacco ties elsewhere at Camp Crazy Horse while he was gone. He shook Smokey back and forth. "Some joke, huh?"

"For me, it is." Smokey spread his hands out, as if to brush away a ghost. "My old lady."

Alex let his whole body sag. Speeding to arrive before the patient died, he'd hoped his first visitor would be an old-timer with a heart attack. Instead it was Dolores DuPree, Smokey's old flame from Lost Dog Creek. The Great Mystery was laughing at Alex's puffed-up pride. "So that's why you're hiding here by the fire pit."

"I can't get rid of her." Smokey hit Alex on the shoulder. "Make her go away."

Alex stifled a laugh. "What's she want?"

"Me! Cuz, she's after me for kid support, but I already gave her my car." Smokey called out to the men around the fire pit. "Get ready for hot rocks and strong prayers for safety inside."

Alex laughed again. "All these brave warriors can't protect you from your ex?" He wanted to jump into the sweat lodge as well, but as the new Turning Hawk medicine man, he had to greet visitors. He watched his AIM warriors undress and disappear into the sweat lodge. "Save me some rocks," he said. Deserted by his buddies. Just when he needed prayers in a relaxing sweat lodge. He yanked the doorflap down and turned away.

"Mabel's keeping her busy in your cabin," Smokey called from inside.

Mabel the camp cook. Baxter's old lady, who was an old lady. Since Alex hadn't eaten all day, he welcomed the idea of her beef stew, frybread and tons of coffee to keep him awake.

But he hesitated. Only four years ago when he'd turned sixteen, Dolores Dupree had tried to snag him at the Rosebud Fair rodeo after he'd won the bareback and roping trophies. He hesitated. At least Mabel would be there. He didn't need to be alone with an old admirer.

Inside his log cabin, Mabel handed him a bowl of stew with frybread. He sat down to eat, then looked around. "Where's Dolores?"

Mabel gestured to the far corner. "Chief-Cook-and-Bottle-Washer gotta watch the men's sweat lodge door." She shut the door tight as she left.

A lump under a pile of blankets, asleep. In his bed.

The blanket pile stirred. "You bring Smokey with you?" Dolores asked. She pushed away the covers, came over to the table, and sat down. She held up a small baby wrapped in a plaid blanket. He remembered the last time he'd seen Dolores: small, drunk and fast. In those days she'd called him Alexina, teasing to get his attention. She'd grabbed for his rodeo trophy buckle, but he'd ducked. With her other hand she'd yanked his black reservation hat off his head and run away, laughing at him and taunting him to catch her. He'd chosen to lose his hat.

Today she was sober, older and worn, her hair frizzed from a bad permanent.

"Hello, *tahanshi*," she said.

Cousin, he thought, but they were very distantly related. She lived over at Lost Dog Creek housing. Before, at rodeos, she'd always called him *boy* but now she was using *cousin* to get close and ask him for something.

He cleared the table and dumped the plates and mugs into the dry sink.

Dolores went over to the bed and laid the baby on it, sat down, then brought out a red bundle wrapped with sage from under her coat and placed it on the kitchen table.

He poured her a mug of coffee from the kettle on the woodstove and set a can of evaporated milk beside the sugar bowl.

She shook her head.

He watched her unwrap a red felt cloth, which held a small Sundance pipe, its red bowl already filled with kinnick-kinnick. She'd brought him a 'filled pipe,' an offering he could not refuse. This was not a quick visit to catch Smokey before his monthly veteran's money ran out. This was a formal request for help. His first request since Old Sam said he was ready to be a full-fledged medicine man, no longer in training.

She handed the pipe across the table to him.

Whenever someone brought a medicine man a filled pipe, in the proper ceremonial way, he had to accept it. So he reached out and took hold of the pipe. "Okay," he said, looking into her eyes, which were full of tears. He lit the pipe and took in long, slow draughts, puffing until the kinnick-kinnick was all gone. He tamped the bowl and shook out the ashes onto a tin plate to take to the sweat lodge altar. Then he asked, "How can The Great Mystery help you?"

She began a tale of woe, Smokey deserting her once he saw the baby, a girl, blaming her for drinking all the time while pregnant. Of course, who was drinking with her? Who was buying the hooch? Him, Smokey. But now, no, he'd quit after his sister died, joined the AIM sober-sides, moved out to Camp Crazy Horse, and she couldn't even get him out of the sweat lodge. He wouldn't even come to the naming, because he called his own daughter *pashicha*—

Alex waited until Dolores caught her breath.

"But she's not deformed."

"What did you name her?" Alex asked.

"Wanakcha. Flower. Because she looks like a prairie flower." Dolores lifted the baby still wrapped in the blanket and thrust her at Alex. "See, look, she's a flower with a round petal face. She's not deformed. *Hiya*, not."

At least this baby was alive, if strangely silent. Alex took the baby in his arms, so tiny, so light, so different from the dead weight of Hokshicala. He guessed she was about six months old. This one scrunched up her eyes but made no sound. All the baby nephews he'd held had been wiggly and squally, a handful to hold, best strapped into their traditional cradleboards. As an only child, he'd had less experience with babies than his AIM brothers and sisters.

"See how good she is! She doesn't even cry!" Dolores pretended to be a proud mother.

She reached out and unwrapped the blanket so he could see the baby's tiny hands and toes. "See, perfect eyes, lots of dark hair, not bald like White babies."

Alex held the baby up before him, wondering about the broad, slightly-flattened face and small size. He wrapped her back in her blanket. "How old is Wanakcha? Was she born early?"

"*Hiya*, not too early, just small like me."

Alex took hold of a tiny finger and shook it. "*Tokiya he?*" What's going on? The baby stared back at Alex. He shook his head, unsure about such a silent infant.

"She doesn't understand Lakota yet," Dolores said.

In the distance he could hear sweat lodge songs, surging with the heat and splashed with cold water. He lifted the glass salt shaker and moved it back and forth in front of Wanakcha, watching the baby's eyes track the shiny glass facets. "But she's a good Lakota baby, watching everything and learning." He handed the baby back to Dolores. "How can I help?"

"I want to put on a ceremony."

"You want to get Smokey back?" He wasn't that kind of medicine man, using Elk Power to catch love. He'd wanted Tate to come with him on her own, and she had, like a whirlwind.

"I know that wouldn't work," Dolores said, "and I don't need him, I have my daughter. My family in Lost Dog Creek don't want Smokey around. They kicked him out after the last big fight." She sighed. "No. I want you to doctor Wanakcha. She's perfect, but she's too quiet. She never cries. Sometimes she gurgles, but babies always cry, all my younger brothers and sisters cried when I took care of them as babies. I know all about babies, left with them all the time when the grownups went out to party."

Then she burst into tears again. "I love Wanakcha as she is, but I know something's not right. Give me some *pejuta wakan* to give her, put into her bottle." Dolores brought out a baby bottle from her handbag.

"You're not nursing?"

Dolores wrinkled up her mouth in distaste. "Oh, no, I always gave my brothers and sisters bottles. And the nurses at the clinic showed me how to sterilize the bottles, and then mix in the formula with boiled water, all clean and sanitary."

Alex wondered if Tate were going to nurse their baby, just as Iná had nursed him—the traditional natural way, close and intimate. Would bottle-fed babies bond with their feeders rather than their mothers, in the same way bottle-fed calves bonded with whoever fed them? Some of his girl cousins bottle-fed their babies, and sometimes added Tylenol to their babies' bottles to get them to sleep through the night—drugged from birth. He hid his thoughts and kept his voice even. "Is Wanakcha quiet because you put Tylenol in her bottle?"

"Oh, no, it's not that. Even when Smokey came to see me in the Pine Ridge Hospital and he got mad and shook her, even then she didn't cry out. So I've kind of known she was different. But I thought she'd grow out of it when I got home to Lost Dog Creek. I mean, I don't mind that she's such a good baby, quiet and lets me sleep through the night, but still—"

"Didn't the nurses or doctor in Pine Ridge say anything?"

Dolores shook her head.

"Didn't they tell you what to do in case Wanakcha is in pain? Maybe she can't cry—no vocal cords. Could she be dumb?"

"She's not dumb, she knows when I'm around. She looks for me in the room."

"I mean mute, born without vocal cords, unable to talk." But Alex knew that even those born without vocal cords could make air noises, could groan and howl.

"They didn't tell me nothing," Dolores shook her head again. "Just go to the baby clinic in Eagle Nest every three months for formula."

The Pine Ridge doctor should have checked Wanakcha for vocal cords. Usually they spanked the baby on delivery to get the newborn to cry and clear the lungs. Surely Wanakcha had cried at birth, or they would have noted it on her chart. Or maybe not. He'd heard there was a new doctor interning on the Res, and the Moccasin Telegraph relayed that he'd been too busy to help some of the elders who appeared at the main clinic unannounced. Alex wondered if that new doctor would be the one to deliver Tate and his baby—or would it be Iná and the midwives?

Alex picked up a metal pan lid and clanged it against the wood-stove. The baby turned to listen, but made no cry. So she wasn't deaf, just not scared by loud noises.

"Well, she isn't deaf," Alex said, "so that's good."

It was Alex's first doctoring ceremony, and all his training in herbs and prayers and people's fears was of little help. A silent non-deaf baby was something new. True, he had little experience with babies. But he hadn't heard of this before, and he doubted there was a sacred herb to cure it. What should he do now? Dolores had brought him the pipe, so he must go through with a ceremony, but he had nothing to give her to cure Wanakcha.

Then he heard Old Sam's words: 'Who is it that must be doctored? Who is not doing well? Give her things to do.' Dolores was not doing well. The mother must be helped. If he gave Dolores herbal tea, she could be free of depression and despair, and Wanakcha would be okay.

He told Dolores four things to prepare for the ceremony:

"Pray while making tobacco ties. Make a guardian spirit hoop to hang over her bed. Hold her so she can hear your heartbeat, as if she were newborn. Then sing to Mother Earth, take her outside and together pick berries, flowers, and sage."

"*Pilamaya,*" she said. Thanks. She left a pouch of Bull Durham tobacco, the traditional gift, on the kitchen table, and went out the door with Wanakcha.

Alex was bothered by Dolores' second request, a naming ceremony for Wanakcha, even though she already had a lovely Lakota name.

He thought about which of her relations would be sober enough to help Dolores prepare.

Old Sam whispered in his ear: 'That might be impossible. Isn't she a DuPree?'

Still, Alex knew that people could change.

He helped Dolores climb in the car and place Wanakcha in the front seat. He held his breath as the old car's engine coughed, belched smoke, and died.

But by the time he'd headed for the sweat lodge, Dolores had teased the engine to fire, backfire, and chug-chug-along the track out past the Sundance grounds toward the gate at the entrance to Camp Crazy Horse. He hoped she'd make it all the way back to Lost Dog Creek housing. And he hoped he could find a way to make baby Wanakcha cry.

Hokshicala, too, had not cried.

CHAPTER 12
TATE

On the road to Porcupine, midmorning

ESCAPE BY fancy car, Tate hoped. But would they ever leave Iná's driveway? After breakfast, she and Dr. Belva had loaded the black briefcase full of blank affidavits, tape recorder, extra tapes and notary public stamp into the back seat. Dressed for business in her suit and heels.

"Get in and fasten your seatbelt," Dr. Belva said.

Res cars didn't have seatbelts. "Where is it?" Tate asked.

Dr. Belva laughed. "Behind your right shoulder. Pull it until you can buckle it into the socket by your left hip. If I need to brake quickly, you won't be thrown into the dashboard. Ready now?" She turned the key and revved the engine.

Not quite. Iná ran down the kitchen steps carrying a bundle in her arms. On top sat a lunch bag and two water bottles. As if they were going on a long-distance safari. Rapping on Tate's window, Iná called, "Open up. No cafés on the way." From her apron pocket she thrust a flashlight into Tate's lap.

"Thanks," said Dr. Belva, who already had one in the glove compartment.

Iná stroked Tate's black leather seat. "Good thing to strap you in." Then she opened the back door and unloaded her bundle: raincoats, blankets, midwife kit with bandages and herbs.

Dr. Belva said, "Just in case, we have a spare tire and jack in the trunk."

Iná pursed her lips and looked overhead at the cloudy day. "Might rain, still spring. Tate, you keep her on the paved roads."

Tate knew what South Dakota gumbo meant: mired in muck. "It's paved all the way."

"Porcupine a long way. Come back before dark," Iná said as Tate rolled up the window.

Dr. Belva Thundercloud drove past Lost Dog Creek and Kyle. The Res roads were nearly deserted except for yellow school buses, college or CAP staff cars, a pickup full of hay bales, a loud motorcycle, and looking backwards, another pickup with big dual tires and deer headlights, following but not passing them.

Dr. Belva looked over at Tate. "I can tell you're smart. Your brain still works. You're bright, you speak well. Why don't you go to college, become a lawyer for your People?"

"I will. First I have to pass my GED test."

Dr. Belva cleared her throat. "Have you studied the booklet?"

"Don't worry, I'll ace the test," Tate said. "I taught dropouts like me at AIM's Little Red School House in Minneapolis how to guess the right answers."

"Good. We need more educated Indian women—they're too few of us now, but at least we can be role models. We had none. We made our own way."

"Iná wants me to be a midwife, but now I want to become a lawyer like you." She tapped Dr. Belva on the shoulder. "So we have to stop here!"

An ultra-modern building stood alone on a hill away from Kyle, a round cement and steel building which swept up as if on eagles' wings, perhaps the visual dream of a foreign architect. Set on the open prairie, it was too far from Pine Ridge's amenities like the café, hospital, housing, and nearby White Clay, Nebraska, liquor stores. It wasn't a regular solid brick BIA-type building with square walls and rooms, with doors which could be closed for privacy. The College Center was based on the round idea of an old-time dance hall or gigantic tipi.

Dr. Belva parked in front of the circle. "Is this the Porcupine Center already?"

"No, this is *Piya Wichoni*, the Oglala Sioux Community College. Which means 'new beginnings.' I can take my GED test and you can use the phone and tour the place, but the staff here is modern, so we won't get any affidavits."

Tate led Dr. Belva into the building and talked first to the receptionist at the door, Velma Brave Elk, in a business suit and permed hair. The modern assimilated women were proud to speak English, and used birth control, despite being Catholic. No chance of affidavits here.

Tate marveled at the busy switchboard lights reaching phones in every office. Velma would be too busy, between constant phone calls, to be helpful, but she might break protocol and let Dr. Belva use a phone line.

When Tate returned, having passed her GED 100%, she found that Velma had taken a break to show off a Navajo lawyer to the President and teachers in their offices. Two successes.

Dr. Belva let her drive to Porcupine. She just fit behind the wheel, shifted smoothly into gear, and drove carefully on the paved road. As they ate Iná's packed lunch in the car, spring rain began to fall. She noticed the same suspicious pickup with a stock rack behind them, but Dr. Belva, after her phone call, didn't seem worried.

"Ignore the guy," Dr. Belva said, "I reached my brother, and he'll watch out for us."

"You're lucky to have a brother." Tate said. "Growing up I had only me—same as Alex."

"I am. We're twins. We think alike. I chose to be a lawyer and use the Law of the Land. He's different. He embraces the Order of the Universe." She smiled. "Perhaps you'll meet him."

When they reached Porcupine, Tate drove to the Porcupine College Center and asked where the WARN meeting was—down the road at the People's Clinic. A hand-painted sign above the door said, 'Women of All Red Nations.' It was National, not just Pine Ridge Reservation.

Marion Red Bear, a strong AIM member, greeted them. "You're the Denver lawyer we've been waiting for. Why didn't you come here first, rather than stop in Eagle Nest?"

Dr. Belva coolly replied, "I thought it appropriate to visit the Midwives' House first, since they are the right generation for collecting evidence."

No, Tate said to herself, it was because I wrote that letter.

Marion introduced the WARN members: the nurses running the women's clinic; the activists for public relations; the angry women with only one child; then the ones coming for the big stew-and-frybread lunch. These younger women wore jeans and sneakers, tee-shirts with AIM logos, jeans jackets embroidered with AIM slogans. Tate recognized several traditionals who'd sundanced at Camp Crazy Horse: Bernice Miller from Kyle, Carla Devereaux from Hisle.

Dr. Belva shook each woman's hand, saying "I'm so glad you're here."

"How did you find us?" Marion asked.

"When I was in law school I followed the news about Wounded Knee '73 and WARN."

Tate kept count of names. In Eagle Nest, the AIM house was run by men but here, closer to Wounded Knee, AIM women had taken charge. They'd started an informal clinic for women who chose not to go to the IPH hospital in Pine Ridge village.

"We've tried to get publicity, but even the AIM warriors aren't interested in our troubles." Marion ended by adding, "The Moccasin Telegraph said you were in Eagle Nest. We were expecting you to come to Porcupine WARN first, where we are ready to help you with the Connie Uri Lawsuit. Do you know Connie Uri?"

Dr. Belva stood next to Marion and said, "My friend Connie Uri, a Native American doctor, discovered a terrible injustice. One of her Native American patients wanted a *womb* transplant. She had consented to a hysterectomy only because she was told the operation was reversible. But it wasn't."

Tate shook her head. Indian Public Health told her that?

Dr. Belva continued, "When Dr. Uri examined Indian Public Health records in Oklahoma, she found that since 1972, three-quarters of the sterilized Indian women hadn't signed consent papers."

"And before then?" Bernice Miller asked. "What about the Boarding School women?"

Tate thought of the midwives at Iná's house, all those older childless women, and Iná with only Alex.

Carla Devereaux asked, "What about Bea Medicine in Wisconsin?

"Yes, we've included her, too. Bertha Medicine Bull found two fifteen-year-old girls on the Cheyenne Res in Montana who thought they'd had appendectomies, but no—they were sterilized for life."

Tate shuddered, thankful she'd canceled her own Indian Public Health appointments.

"Worse, said Dr. Belva. "We have data from Arizona, New Mexico, and South Dakota."

Marion Red Bear asked, "You've heard of our efforts here with Senator Abourezk?"

"Yes, we know. Senator Abourezk demanded a full GAO Congressional report."

Bernice Miller hmpfed. "Another Bureau like the BIA: Boss Indian Around."

Dr. Belva replied, "Yes, the GAO. General Accounting Office. They do more than audits. Last year they interviewed the guy responsible for all the sterilization, Dr. Emery Johnson, Director of the Indian Health Service. He justified their policy of non-therapeutic sterilization, calling it 'family planning.' Meaning, planning for zero Indian families!"

"You mean Genocide?" Echoes around the room.

"Yes," said Dr. Belva.

"You know what that BIA bastard said?" Bernice Miller spit out the words: "We are not aware of any instance in which such services have been abused."

Dr. Belva added, "The Committee found that 3,400 Native American women were sterilized without informed consent. Maybe a quarter of them are here on Pine Ridge. I am here to prove him wrong!"

Tate was silent. Maybe that was why her mother-in-law hated Indian Public Health so much. Maybe that's why Iná had only one child. No wonder Iná had sent her off with Dr. Belva -to spare the midwives and others in Eagle Nest from being interviewed, answering questions, and signing affidavits. No wonder Iná was so sensitive—not just that it wasn't talked about, but that it was shameful and all this time the Indian women had thought being unable to have children was their own fault.

As if Tate had spoken aloud, Dr. Belva added, "We have no idea how many were sterilized in the fifties and sixties, when the files were conveniently 'transferred' or lost. It's those older women with only one child, or none at all, that I'm looking for."

The very ones who won't talk. Carla Devereau asked, "What good will interviews do?"

"Interviews lead to affidavits for our lawsuit," Dr. Belva added.

Marion Red Bear stood. "You have affidavits?"

"Oh, yes." Tate handed her the papers from Dr. Belva's briefcase.

"We need witnesses," said Dr. Belva.

"Evidence!" Bernice cried.

"Signed statements," Carla added.

Dr. Belva stood up. "Yes, all that. Then we sue. We file a Class Action lawsuit. While your men fight for our abrogated treaties of the Great Sioux Nation, we women will bring lawsuits to win our rights."

Marion took charge. "Susie, run over to the College Center to make more copies for us." Grateful for a coffee break, Dr. Belva Thundercloud distributed a set of questions for each interview from her black briefcase:

1. Did you go to an IPH doctor for your first child? Date, name, location.
2. Were you put under anesthesia?
3. Did they ever give you birth control methods: pill, IUD, rhythm, etc.?
4. Did they ask you if you wanted a tubal ligation? Or explain it?
5. When did you discover that you couldn't get pregnant again?
6. Did you go to an IPH doctor to find out what was wrong?
7. Did they tell you that you had your tubes tied and could never "untie" them? Did they tell you that you'd been sterilized forever?

Tate, feeling self-important, recorded their stories, marked each tape with date, time and location. If forced to, could she explain in Lakota? Enough to get good answers? She needed a Lakota language class for herself—with a woman, to learn women's words and grammatical endings, which were different from the men's. But they hadn't reached the older generation.

During the coffee break, WARN members brought in older women and Dr. Belva collected their stories. Tate marked each woman's name on a coded index card, giving only number, date, and location. Then she set up the tape recorder and filed the statements in folders from Belva's briefcase.

WARN wanted to keep Dr. Belva in Porcupine, but she declined gracefully to head back to Eagle Nest. Marion replied, "Well, then, we will do your work here in the southwest part of Pine Ridge Res. You in Eagle Nest take the northeast and Rosebud Res."

Dr. Belva was very happy—many affidavits.

Tate was very happy, having mastered note cards and tape recorder. A successful day!

"Whew," Dr. Belva said. "Did you see how they grabbed onto me? They've been dealing with a lot of injustices. I'm exhausted. Let's escape to Wounded Knee. You say it's only ten miles south, and the road's still paved, so rain isn't a problem."

Tate loved driving the elegant car with such smooth handling, rain or no rain. She asked, "Was this lawsuit part of Wounded Knee '73?"

Dr. Belva replied, "Oh, yes. The involuntary sterilization of Indian women was one of the reasons *for* the Occupation. That's why so many women went inside to protest." Dr. Belva paused. "You must have been twelve or thirteen then?"

Tate's friend Joanna Joe had gone inside. "I lived in Minneapolis then, working at AIM's Little Red Schoolhouse with the kids. Where were you?"

"Law school. If I'd gone, I'd have lost my internship." Dr. Belva paused. "Did any of your relatives suffer here?"

"No idea. All I know is my birth date and that my Lakota birth mother named me Tate. I hate to go to Pine Ridge Village. Someone might look just like me, and what could be worse, finding no trace, or finding she's there?"

"Perhaps your Turning Hawk relatives would know."

Iná, of course, who four years ago tried to keep Alex away from Wounded Knee.

To fill a silence that followed, Tate said, "There's not much left, just a burned-out store, church, and the cemetery." She drove past the official Cemetery's arched entrance with flags on the right, but stopped at the ravine on the left. Now chokecherry and wild plum were starting to bloom, alongside a rivulet of fresh water. Hidden among tall grasses were faded red tobacco ties, silent prayers left by many who remembered those who died that day. The red tobacco ties she'd placed there last year as an offering were faded now after the winter storms.

"Here's where it happened," Tate said. "After Sitting Bull's murder in December, 1890, Big Foot led his band on a trail south to escape to Wounded Knee Village. On arrival the U.S. Army drove them into a ravine. Over three hundred men, women, and children were massacred."

"I don't need to see another mass grave, Belva replied. "Rain melts our tears and we turn weak." She rolled up the window. "We Navajo have our own tragic history, older than yours. When The Long Walk to Bosque Redondo began, men, women, and children marched over three hundred miles. More than three hundred also died. Drive on.

What I want to see is the Resistance I missed while in law school: the AIM Occupation of Wounded Knee four years ago."

So Tate stopped on the left at Gildersleeve's burned-out storefront—once full of Lakota artifacts—which AIM had used as infirmary and kitchen. Dr. Belva walked across the road toward the grassy hill in front of the battered Catholic Church. Tate caught up with her and showed her the circular rings still in the grass where Crow Dog had built his tipi and sweat lodge out in the open—defying the Army to send bullets to bounce off their spiritual center.

"I don't want to see inside the church," said Dr. Belva. "I want to see the trenches where the AIM warriors held their ground." So they walked past the tribal housing onto the hillocks of open prairie. Logs and car hoods once covered where AIM warriors had slept and fought.

CHAPTER 13

ALEX

Camp Crazy Horse, late morning

AS THE prairie grass emerged, the earth softened so much the AIM warriors could no longer haul more logs from the pines. Instead, they trimmed the ones they had and began building cabins for a year-round camp. Tired and hungry, Alex led them back to the big cabin for the noon meal that Mabel had cooked.

At the door Mabel handed Alex a swaddled bundle. "Here! This one don't cry. Dolores left Wanakcha for you, said your medicine don't work."

Alex, his hands still dirty from peeling logs, held Wanakcha in his arms without touching the blanket. What was he to do?

"She said her Lost Dog Creek relatives kicked her out and she has nowhere to go, so she can't raise her baby, but I know her type—she just went directly to Interior Bar to get passed-out drunk so she won't be able to remember what she did."

"That chicken-shit bitch snuck into camp when we wouldn't be around," said Smokey.

"I hear this one's yours!" Mabel said.

"She's got your smoky eyes," Old Louie added.

"That's what you get for tipi-crawling," put in Chaské.

Sonny pulled up his shirt and kneaded his man-breasts. "Better get your tits ready."

Without a word Smokey grabbed the baby from Alex and bolted out the door. Alex heard the camp pickup start and rev up. He ran out to block Smokey. "*Kolá*, wait!"

"She's gonna get it back!" Smokey turned the pickup around.

Alex leapt forward, yanked the passenger door open, and slid onto the seat beside the baby. He wrested the stick shift from Smokey into neutral. "Look at your daughter. Do you really want to take her to Interior Bar? We can keep her here at Camp Crazy Horse."

Smokey revved the engine in idle while they sat in place, then shook his head. "I can't keep her. My mother won't have her. We got no relatives here, only urban Indians off in LA."

Alex turned off the engine. "*Kolá*, we'll go inside, keep the baby warm beside the stove, then eat and talk like men."

Inside, the men sat down to eat while Mabel took the quiet baby. "She needs a change. That drunk didn't leave nothing for the baby, no bottle, no clothes, no diapers. Got old rags?"

Alex found a clean dishtowel and handed it to Mabel.

She laid Wanakcha on Alex's workbench, unwrapped the bundle, and shrieked.

"Eh?" Badger said. "You forgot how babies look?"

Mabel burst into wild yelps and thrust the naked baby up away from her for all to see. Pee arced over the workbench onto the floor. "Dolores been tricking you. Wanakcha is a boy."

Alex couldn't believe what was before his eyes. How could he not have known? He flushed. Dolores had tricked him as well. Did she think she'd get more pity with a baby girl? Then when that didn't work, that Smokey wouldn't abandon a son?

Old Louie broke the silence. "That's some medicine power you got, Alex, overnight changing a girl into a boy!"

Alex laughed. "Smokey, you get to name your son after all!"

"Let's call him 'Left Behind,'" said Chaské.

"*Wihepeya.*" Given-away.

"*Cheya-shni.*" No-cry.

"*Wablenicha.*" Orphan.

"*Wanakcha-shni.*" Wanakcha-not. Mabel handed him the diapered and swaddled boy.

Smokey sat stunned with the silent baby in his lap.

"Stop!" Alex, thinking of Hokshicala, called out to get the warriors to stop joshing. "This baby boy can have lots of nicknames, but since he was left here on the land, the land will give him a name. We'll go into the sweat, not too hot, and pray to *Tunkashila,* the Great Mystery."

Alex went into the sweat first, carrying the deer antlers, then Smokey carrying the silent baby in his lap. The rest of the AIM warriors ducked and sat around the circle. Chaské carried in the glowing rocks, seven for an easy sweat, then climbed in by the door and pulled the flap shut. In the darkness Alex poured on water. As the rocks hissed and steam filled their lungs, they filled the lodge with first-round songs. Alex prayed to *Tunkashila,* then took the baby from Smokey, unwrapped him, held him high over the hissing rocks, *tunke oyate,* the born-and-ancient ones, letting the steam wrap around the baby's body. When he felt the baby stirring, he lifted him back into his lap and rubbed sage gently all over his tiny body. Then he wrapped him up again and gave him to Smokey.

Alex felt Smokey next to him, shaking, rocking back and forth, overcome with emotion. Then Smokey broke down and howled above the ancient songs, like the grief and pain of a mare losing a newborn colt to wolves.

Alex and the others sang even louder, to cover Smokey's sobbing, since the sacred sweat lodge was the only place a grown man could cry without shame. When the song ended, Alex opened the door flap and in the filtered light motioned the others to leave Smokey and baby in the sweat.

Outside, Alex closed the door flap securely. "Short sweat," he said. "Out of respect, we'll leave Smokey with the Great Mystery, who alone can comfort him."

Alex wondered, had Dolores been playing a trick on him to see if a real medicine man could tell whether a swaddled baby was a boy or a girl? Had she wanted to test Smokey? Had she wanted a girl and pretended, or deluded herself? Whatever, he'd been fooled.

As they dressed and walked back toward the big cabin for dinner, Alex stopped to listen. In the distance he heard his hawk calling from the pines, "kree–kree–" and closer by, another sharp cry. Two cries. A low deep sobbing, and above it, a high-pitched mewling. Alex turned back, amazed and humbled. His heart swelled. The prayers for the baby that didn't cry had been answered; now the rest was up to the father—and the Camp.

When Smokey emerged and stood in the doorway of the big cabin, he held his son to his chest, rocking him. "His name is Jerome Junior. My real name."

Who knew the power of the Great Mystery? Word of the two miracles—a girl changed into a boy and mute baby instantly cured—spread around the Res. Because of Alex's new miracles, many came to the camp expecting to be fed and take sweat, so that the camp almost ran out of food and firewood.

Alex needed Tate at the Camp. Preoccupied, he headed to his cabin for peace and quiet. As he came near, he noticed a shadow covering the red hand painted years ago by his grandpa: the welcome sign of a chief's tipi. The shadow became distinct: black tobacco ties, more this time, threatening his home and Camp Crazy Horse. Someone was walking on Turning Hawk land, invisible like a *wanaghi*, a ghost stalking him.

Not his father, Até. Someone else was trying to destroy the Turning Hawk family. A taller older cowboy was still standing there, fiddling with the black ties.

Outraged, Alex bounded onto the man's back and forced him to the ground. He grabbed the black tobacco tie from the man's gloved hand, but before he could toss the tie into the fire pit nearby, he was flipped over and pinned beneath a much stronger stranger.

"Whoa," the man said, sitting on Alex's chest. "Belva Thundercloud sent me."

The Denver lawyer staying at Iná's. The one Tate called "Dr. Belva," a Navajo. Alex struggled to roll free from the man's muscled arms and kick the man's back. Then lay still, at the ready to head-punch and twist away. Above him hovered an Indian with a red headband, black ponytail, silver concho belt, moccasins: another Navajo on the Res. Maybe he was AIM as well.

"*Kola!*" the man called, added something in Navajo, then English: "My name is Ben."

Kola was the Lakota word for *buddy*. Was he AIM or traditional? Or both, like himself? Alex sucked in enough air to bellow, "My name is Alex. Why were you meddling with those black tobacco ties?"

Ben stood up to let Alex rise. "When I recognized the Red Hand of Welcome, I decided to remove the Evil Ones." With his glove he wrapped the black ties in a kerchief. "We don't burn or bury Evil, we simply leave. What is your tradition?"

Alex pondered the idea that you could simply '*leave Evil.*' To move away and leave the Land, rather than drive Evil out, burn Evil up, or bury Evil in Mother Earth. Or drown Evil in the Ocean, which he'd never seen. He'd examine these ideas later when he'd go on

Hanblechia to face the Great Mystery. He threw the kerchief of black ties into the firepit's glowing coals. "I like to burn," he said, "but my mother chooses to bury."

When the coals died down, he led Ben Thundercloud into his log cabin. Mabel had left the enamel coffeepot on the woodstove to boil down, filling the air with burned grounds. It didn't matter. This had been a great day—two miracles and a new friend. He and Ben sat at the table, drank cold clear stream water, and rolled Bull Durham smokes. After a comfortable silence, he asked Ben, "Why are you here?"

"She called me. My sister Belva, the Denver lawyer, is in danger. It's the sterilization lawsuit. Someone has followed her since she left the airport and drove to the Res." He rolled another smoke. "Just to let you know, I'm shadowing your wife Tate as well."

Whom he'd not seen in days, since those two had been driving around Porcupine. "How are they doing?"

"While you're busy with *visitors* and the search for whoever is hexing Turning Hawk land and Camp Crazy Horse, they're collecting evidence at the Women of All Red Nations and even been to Wounded Knee. My sister lets your wife drive on the bumpy gravel roads."

Alex laughed. "How can you keep up with them, out of sight? Are you a Detective? Or a sheep rancher?"

"I am *haatali.* I live in the shadows."

Alex had heard of such Navajo night singers, a different kind of medicine healing.

"My sister and I are twins. We think alike. It's different from your 'Moccasin Telegraph.' She works with the Law for Justice; I work with the Songs for Healing."

CHAPTER 14
TATE

Ina's House, morning

WHEN TATE woke up and went into the kitchen to sneak two cups of delicious Res coffee, she realized the house was empty. So was the gravel driveway outside. Both Dr. Belva's rental car and Iná's Midwife Express were gone. Only Grandma Agatha was sitting at the dining room table, piecing another baby quilt.

Blood rushed to Tate's head. How could this have happened? This was to be Belva and Tate's second day to collect affidavits. Left behind with only Grandma Agatha, the oldest midwife. Left behind with Iná's To-Do List on the kitchen counter. In secret Iná had stolen Belva away, ordering her new Very-Important-Person to drive to—

"Grandma," Tate asked, sitting down next to her, "where'd they go?"

"Most likely Rosebud, more relations over there, Parmelee, Upper Cut Meat, Soldier Creek, St. Francis Mission."

That meant Iná and her midwives would be gone all day, maybe taking pots and pans for a night meeting ceremony, which meant: see you in the morning. The more Tate seethed inside, the quieter the house echoed. She rushed downstairs to find the other midwives gone, too. They must have caravanned together.

The old ladies would come back saying that they'd gone to pick sweetgrass at Ring Thunder, but Tate knew they'd stop at the Rosebud Tribal Office and the Sinté Gleshka College for lunch to show off the Navajo woman lawyer instead.

"So I'm stuck here all day when I could be getting women to sign affidavits," Tate said. She didn't say, *stuck with you*. Instead, she asked, "Why did they leave you behind?"

Grandma Agatha said nothing.

So Tate answered her own question, "So you could watch over me in case I wanted to sneak away to my husband?"

"Not really." Grandma Agatha took off her apron. "Haven't you noticed?"

Grandma Agatha always wore dark dresses. But today she was engulfed by a huge Hawaiian beach shirt decorated with palm trees, people swimming in the surf, others sunbathing under a big umbrella.

"My favorite tent," she said. "I thought you might enjoy seeing it."

Tate opened her mouth—and closed it.

"I had a coconut once, round and hairy," Grandma Agatha continued. "It fell from a tree right at my feet, and my admirer popped its bellybutton open with a screwdriver so we could drink the sweet juice together."

So in her heyday Grandma Agatha had been to Florida, or maybe Hawaii—with a man. But in the Midwife House, she could never wear it—except now, when Tate would never tell. Yet this old midwife had remembered how much it meant to be with your man.

Grandma Agatha handed her a frybread. "About your mother-in-law. She lets you call her *Iná*, mother, not mother-in-law. It's an honor. When she scolds you, she doesn't call you *Takosh*, daughter-in-law, she calls you Tate. She likes you, but she'll never show it."

Tate hugged Grandma Agatha, who'd guessed Tate hadn't had a real mother. Her foster mother had called her Tatiana, pretending she was a Hungarian princess, and her birth mother was unknown. But for how long could she bear such an honorable mother—for the rest of her life? She might as well bear it. When Iná returned, she would claim her fate: "I take you as my real mother." And like a real mother, Iná had left one midwife to watch over her because she might go into labor, even though it was only her eighth month.

Grandma Agatha smiled. "If you finish your *chekpa ognake* before Iná returns, you win."

Yes, Tate could finish the beaded turtle bag for her baby girl before Iná finished hers for a baby boy. Grandma Agatha had noticed their stubborn competition.

She also said, "If Iná wins, you can keep yours for a baby girl next time."

Afterwards, Tate invited Flossie and Buster over to hear her play the piano. Then all four of them sat at the dining table to eat soup and bread the midwives had made. Soon it was dark, and Flossie and Buster went home. How often would they be able come back, if only for food?

Then Grandma Agatha set a chair in place for Tate, pulled the blinds down, turned the lights off, and lit a candle. She'd chosen a traditional way to tell a story. Tate sat very still as Grandma Agatha pulled their chairs close. It felt like an initiation. Tate stopped beading.

Her elder, Grandma Agatha, who was called "Old Lady Little Thunder," rocked in her chair and spoke. "I stayed to tell you the story of *Chekpa Ognake*. So you and your mother-in-law stop quarreling. Not good to quarrel just before the baby's born."

Tate had heard that old name before. "I don't know much Lakota yet."

Grandma Agatha laughed. "I do speak English."

Chekpa Ognake

"Long time ago many babies died at birth. One day a medicine woman came and said, "We lose too many babies. When they take their first breath into this world, we must protect them so they choose to stay with us. So we must keep their cord of life for nine months.

"You must save the cord, wash it to let it dry. Then wrap it in clean moss, put it in small pouch, and tie it to the top of the cradleboard so the baby will see and remember you the mother. This way, the baby will not think to return to Spirit World and leave you to weep and mourn. This world is a cold, hard, and straight Red Road, so sometimes a baby wants to return.

"You cut the pouch from soft deerskin for strong protection. For a boy, bead black and white beads for a lizard, quick and fast. For a girl, bead green and brown beads for a turtle, long life and wise.

"*Chekpa Ognake*—very sacred. The Lizard and Turtle People lived long ago, so strong they turned themselves into Stone People. They live now in the Badlands, proof of long life and power. They're our relatives, like the sweat lodge rocks.

"When your baby crawls out of the cradleboard and walks, then tie the tiny pouch to your baby's dress or coat, always near your baby until grown up, so your child is connected to you always, and remembers our Mother Earth.

"Babies without a pouch for protection feel lost in this world, open to disease and infection. They can be lost, or die, and not even mourned.

"So the ceremony to make *chekpa ognake* is very important for you to prepare for birth, as important as childbirth breathing and making of baby clothes and cradleboard. You must work in group of women, old and young, who already know how to make beaded lizard and turtle pouches. They will help you with cutting, sewing, and design. Each child born must have his or her own beaded pouch, for just as each child is unique, so is each birth cord, *chekpa ognake*."

In the silence afterwards Tate felt humbled. She appreciated Grandma Agatha, so often silent, yet who knew the old remedies and stories. How often had Tate defied Iná, bound to her mother-in-law whether she liked her or not. Now she understood that Iná and the other midwives had sacred tasks to fulfill. They believed birthing was a matter of life or death, and that it was very important to prepare in a sacred rather than trivial way. She was lucky that they would help her prepare and deliver her baby.

No wonder the birth cord, *chekpa ognake,* was so important that women made beaded lizard or beaded turtle bags for their children to wear all through childhood as protection. Tate could hardly wait to share the story. Or not. Too often she gushed with words about something private. No, she would share only with Alex. She missed him, especially after hearing rumors that his first patient didn't even show up for the healing ceremony.

Tate and Grandma's peaceful silence was broken by the caravan's return of Dr. Belva's rental car and Iná's Midwife Express, living up to its name. Pots and pans had been left in the station wagon for washing on the morrow.

Then, surprise—another car pulled into the driveway. Grandma Florence, daughter Francine, and granddaughter Chi-Chi had followed the caravan from Corn Creek to stay overnight, having heard of Alex's great healing powers.

Iná led the relatives into the living room to sleep on couches and chairs. Tate brought sheets, blankets, and pillows up from the basement, and everyone got comfortable for the night.

Smothered in blankets, Grandma Florence cackled and joked around with Iná in Lakota.

"Your daughter-in-law's so big, looks like it'll be twins, and you'll need two cradleboards."

Tate understood most of the joke, and sat down to hide her stomach with extra pillows.

Iná replied, "Tomorrow we see about that, one or two, boy or girl."

"Alex told me only the Great Mystery can tell," Tate said.

Iná hee-heed and Grandma Florence cackled some more. "We know better," they cried, "and tomorrow the ancient ceremony will let us know."

It sounded like fun. Tate asked, "Can I go, too?"

Iná frowned. "Not allowed."

"But why? I'm the one who needs to know."

"Too pregnant." Subject closed.

It didn't matter. Tate made sure that tomorrow they'd scour the Res to find more women to sign affidavits. This time she had the key.

CHAPTER 15

ALEX

Camp Crazy Horse, morning

WORD SPREAD like wildfire about Alex's "miraculous" cure. Alex wished the stories—from getting a silent baby to cry or changing a baby's sex—would stop. If only he could go back to when he was just a medicine-man-in-training and not responsible for what happened. He'd done his best, he'd prayed strong prayers, and it was the Great Mystery who made healings happen. Yet his reputation had grown overnight. He could hardly get time to work on the log cabins for the camp. His pickup was needed to cut and peel saplings for the camp's unfinished tipis. And he must find who had left Hokshicala in the black cradleboard.

He got up before dawn to say his prayers, but there were loud bang-cough-bangs floating down to the Camp from the gate. Before he could finish his prayers he saw a low-slung Nova, glowing yellow-green, coming past the AIM warriors' tipis surrounding the Sundance grounds. He sighed. No one else on the Res, or even the next Res, had a car that color besides Grandma Florence in Rosebud. 'Char-treuse' she called it. His cousin Veronica must be behind the wheel, roused from sleep to drive. Something urgent. No escape from a one-room cabin.

He ducked inside before they could see him and put away his pipe. Indian hospitality meant Grandma Florence must be fed, even if she'd eaten already, and his wife wasn't here, but fortunately he knew how to cook. At the sink he mixed powdered eggs with water and canned beef in a skillet. Usually on the Res when a car pulled in, people waited until someone came to the door, often to call off the camp dogs before welcoming them in. At the solid thump on the door, he called out, "*Tima hiyupo.*" Y'all come in. Must be urgent.

Grandma Florence stepped in with her big traveling diaper bag and looked around. "Grandson, you wearing the apron strings today?" She'd wrapped her white braids around her head like a crown. Behind her, his cousin Veronica carried her two-year-old daughter Chi-Chi bundled in a pink blanket. Veronica had dark circles under her eyes and disheveled hair. Had Chi-Chi kept her awake nights? Did she think her baby was ill? Probably they'd come to him for a doctoring.

Grandma Florence began. "We come to see you after we visit your wife in town."

He drew back, puzzled. Why had they come so early? Had they stayed overnight in town and had his mother sent them to check on him?

They shook his hand formally, even Chi-Chi, who stretched her tiny hand out from her blanket, as people did when they came with a request.

But first they must eat. "*Wanna, wota!*" Alex motioned them to sit down at the red oilcloth-covered table, setting it with plates, forks, left-over frybread and cups of coffee.

Cousin Veronica handed Chi-Chi to Grandma Florence, who sat down at the head of the table. Without a word, Veronica took over the sizzling fry pan. Alex gave her a grateful look and sat down opposite his grandma. Chi-Chi immediately reached out to grab the salt shaker.

She didn't seem sick, merely hungry. Alex reached behind him for a box of commodity raisins and handed it across the table to Grandma Florence. "Is Chi-Chi ill?"

"Oh, no." Grandma Florence shook the box of raisins and handed several to the toddler. "We come to you to find out if your wife carries a boy baby or a girl baby. The ancient way, you remember—or maybe you don't remember, you were only two when your father took you over to Blackpipe Camp to see Old Man Red Leaf. We waited for you to pick the bow and arrows. I was there." She nodded her head and smiled.

He relaxed. Nothing urgent after all. Alex hadn't heard this story of his childhood before. He'd have to check with his mother to see if it was true, or if his grandma was joshing him as she had since he was little, her way of showing affection. But he knew the old Lakota custom: it was believed that medicine men could predict the sex of the baby by offering a child about two years old a choice: to grab a sewing awl or a bow and arrow. If the child chose the awl, the baby would be a girl; if the child chose the bow and arrow, it would be a boy. Only someone like Grandma Florence would keep such old-time traditional toys passed down from one generation to the next.

She continued, "Instead you reached out with both hands, grabbing the small bone awl in your left and the tiny bow and arrows with your right. How we laughed, and Old Man Red Leaf said you would be a greedy one, grabbing for all the knowledge of the old ways." She laughed. "Still, you weren't shy, so we knew your right hand was the right one, the one that counted."

Grandma Florence reached across and tapped his chest. "Now, twenty years later, you're the medicine man. We bring you a small awl and tiny bow and arrows. You must lay them out on a baby star quilt in front of Chi-Chi and let her choose. Only then will your mother be satisfied."

Alex winced. "My mother is never satisfied." Then he remembered the second part of the prophecy: in front of a pregnant woman, if the two-year-old was shy, the baby would be a girl; if the two-year-old was outgoing, it would be a boy. Perhaps he would be saved from this request. He said, "But you must bring both Iná and Tate along, or they won't believe in this prophecy."

Grandma Florence smiled. "A house full of midwives, lots of trouble! Your wife and mother both make a beaded pouch for the new baby's umbilical cord, they argue all day long. Your wife makes one with a beaded turtle, sure the baby is a girl. Your mother makes one with a beaded lizard, sure the baby is a boy. We come here to settle it traditional Lakota way."

His mother and his wife quarreled about everything. He'd heard their current quarrel was whether the unborn baby was a boy or a girl. He made a point to stay out of women's business. His baby would be born, regardless of a beading contest. His mother must have sent Grandma Florence to settle the most recent quarrel.

Luckily Grandma Florence hadn't brought them with her. The day had hardly begun, and though his mother rose at dawn, his very pregnant wife slept late. "I'll wait until you bring both my mother and my wife to see with their own eyes, or they won't believe."

"Oh, no, your mother sent your wife away with that Navajo lawyer, so Tate wouldn't be able to come. But she coming separate," Grandma said, "in her black hearse, with her cane."

Alex shook his head. He must have temporarily lost his hearing. Twenty feet away outside the cabin door sat his mother grim-faced in her Midwife Express. Another huff. Probably Iná had commented about the gaudy car, unwilling to ride in the back of a chartreuse Nova.

His devious Grandma Florence must have had arranged it all. And afterward she'd corner him to learn how he'd managed to buy Tate a fancy new car. Grandma wouldn't ask, just hint around that he should take *her* for a ride around town in that shiny black Mercedes.

Grandma Florence must have understood. From her big diaper bag she took out a small handmade eight-pointed star quilt and said, "We put a baby quilt down for Chi-Chi to sit on. Afterwards, either way, the star quilt's for you."

He couldn't refuse the traditional honoring gift. "*Ohan*. Yes." Tate would be happy, even if she wouldn't be here to see. Grandma Florence had been equally cunning in sewing the star quilt with alternating pink and blue diamonds. Alex could see no way out of the dispute.

He should have prayed harder for a good day.

He picked up his sacred pipe and pouch of kinnik-kinnik, sacred tobacco, and eagle feather for the ceremony by smoke and prayer. Regardless of petty feuds, it was proper to wait for all present to enter together into a sacred space. Even with a chill in the air.

So he led Grandma Florence, carrying Chi-Chi, and Cousin Veronica to the small Turning Hawk Ceremony House, a simple cedar log cabin, built by his grandpa: one door, two windows, three benches along the walls, and in the center a wood stove. His mother, who'd extricated herself from her black station wagon, in her usual black dress and shoes, leaned on her diamond willow cane to assert her authority and followed behind.

He unlatched the door and said, "*Wana*." Now. "We enter this sacred space in peace." He led Grandma Florence and Chi-Chi over the threshold. Cousin Veronica and Iná followed, sitting together on the bench on the women's side.

He closed the door. This was a daylight ceremony, carried on by the women, so preparing a gopher hill altar was unnecessary. He laid his pipe, pouch and eagle feather on the empty wood stove. Everyone sat on the women's side benches.

Grandma Florence handed Chi-Chi to Iná—probably a peace gesture, and laid the small eight-pointed star quilt down in front of the wood stove. It gleamed in the dim light, near where Alex usually made his altar.

Waiting nearby were five cans filled with gopher hill dirt, sacred because gophers see in the dark when they go underground and know the roots for doctoring. Four contained a red cloth flag tied onto a stick, one for each of the four directions. He pushed the last can behind the altar to save for making his round dirt altar for a night-time ceremony.

Then he heard another car zoom down from the Gate into Camp Crazy Horse. Hopefully Smokey or Baxter would greet them by the Sundance grounds, and have them wait.

Grandma Florence, Iná and Veronica sat up, expectant. Even Chi-Chi listened. Was someone else coming? Would the ceremony be interrupted? Or held off for completion?

Alex went over to open the door. A black Mercedes bounced over the rutted road, past the big log cabin, and pulled in behind the Midwife Express. Tate opened the driver side door and got out, her long hair blowing loose in the wind. She'd wrapped her arms across her stomach, as if she knew he'd be angry.

On the other side, Belva the Denver lawyer got out as well. This was the first time he'd seen her, the woman who'd taken over Tate as a secretary. Tall and imposing. Older, dignified, even in a strange situation. Quietly observing, as she would be in a Navajo setting.

The two walked together toward the Ceremony House. If only it had been a serious nighttime doctoring ceremony, when the windows were covered and the door nailed shut. His mother would be furious. So he focused on Grandma Florence, since it was her ceremony, gesturing with his hands, what to do?

"Two more to witness is good," she said.

Of course. It was the black Mercedes she'd wangle a ride in later. He opened the door and retreated to the far side of the room.

Just in time before the ceremony door closed, Grandma Florence took Belva's hand and pulled her to sit down beside her. Belva sat down next to the elder, which left Tate to sit next to Iná. He knew his wife couldn't bear the thought of being nudged by Iná in the belly, her mouth pursed in a tight pout because her daughter-in-law had disobeyed the rules.

Instead, Tate came towards him and sat at the men's benches, breaking another unspoken custom. Too late now to escort her back to sit next to Dr. Belva to explain what was going on. He watched her sit back and tuck her feet in, hoping to look small.

When everyone had settled and quiet filled the room, Grandma Florence sat Chi-Chi in the center of the star quilt, facing Alex. He knelt in front of Chi-Chi and placed the tiny bone awl and wooden bow and arrows in front of her. Then he backed off a few steps.

Chi-Chi cried, turned and crawled toward her mama, who picked her up, shushed her, and gave her sweetgum to chew.

"All of you go outside," Alex ordered. "Leave Chi-Chi alone so she won't get distracted and can concentrate." After the women, including Tate, went outside to look in the windows, Alex lifted Chi-Chi up from Grandma Florence and put her back down on the star quilt.

Chi-Chi looked up at her grandma, and then at the bone and wood toys. Uninterested. Chi-Chi turned around, waved her hands, and giggled. She crawled off the star quilt toward the cans of gopher hill dirt. Kicking and wiggling, she reached out for the bright red flags.

Cousin Veronica rushed in and grabbed Chi-Chi before she could knock anything over. Iná, Belva, and Tate stood in the doorway, unable to tell what had happened.

Grandma Florence laughed. "Well, I guess Chi-Chi, just like you, grandson, didn't choose the ordinary way. All we know is that your baby will become a medicine person!"

Alex was pleased. If only his other *visitors* would leave so happy. Now the stalemate between his wife and mother would wait until the day of his child's birth, a child that would grab for *luta*, the sacred red, not *sha*, the red of ordinary things.

"Aiee!" cried Grandma Florence, pursing her lips at Chi-Chi.

Chi-Chi had picked up a piece of licorice? No, an insect, not a hairy spider, but a black beetle, and was about to—

Both Alex and Grandma Florence rushed toward Chi-Chi, Grandma Florence crying, "No, no, don't eat it!" She lifted the child up and Alex grabbed the black object from her mouth.

A black tobacco tie.

Who had put it there? Why hadn't he seen it earlier? All the black tobacco ties hexing Turning Hawk land and family. Put on Hokshicala in the Vision Cave. In the basement of the Church. Over Grandpa's red hand by the door to the big cabin. Now this.

Grandma Florence and Iná battled in Lakota over whose fault this was: his, his wife's pregnant presence, her sitting on the men's side that had brought it in, or was it the addition of a Navajo who'd witnessed such a shameful, ruined ceremony?

But something else had angered his Rosebud relatives. Veronica wrapped a crying Chi-Chi in the pink and blue blanket and stood by the door. "Cousin," she muttered, "We heard that a Turning Hawk baby lay dead in the Pine Ridge Morgue, yours, but we didn't believe it—"

But she did. She'd taken the pink and blue quilt back. Dishonor to show dishonor.

Iná stopped mid-breath. "Lies and black ties, evil out to destroy Turning Hawk Honor."

Grandma Florence stared at the empty floor where the black tie had been found. Then she, Veronica, and Chi-Chi left in silence.

Only Iná, Tate and Belva remained behind.

~~~

How quickly disaster had arrived. No more 'visitors.' All would stay away from Camp Crazy Horse and Turning Hawk land. The Ceremony House would be condemned. Reputation lost in an instant. He dropped the black tie in an empty tin can, lit a match and watched it burn.

His mother spoke first, in Lakota: "Now all Rosebud will hear about black ties. And how another Turning Hawk baby is dead in Pine Ridge Morgue. Not safely buried in our cemetery?"

Tate understood enough Lakota to flash her eyes at him. "Is it true, what they say, that dead baby was yours? From a shack-up who killed him and left him in the Vision Cave?"

"*Hiya!*" No! Iná answered from the doorway. "My only grandson is inside you!"

"Imagine!" Tate shouted at Alex, "It's a first, your mother defending me!"

He was tired from no sleep, and now both his mother and wife had turned on him. "You interrupted the ceremony, Tate. Now you must help me wash the floor and windows, while I smudge the Ceremony House with cedar and sweetgrass."

"Certainly. This way it will keep all those young mothers away from you."

Alex replied, "No, it keeps me from finding out where Hokshicala's mother is."

A raucous cry, sharp as an eagle bone whistle, pierced the air. Like calling sheep. Belva walked toward him. Copal smoke arose from a small tin, filling the room. "Come," she sang. "We must take hands, all four of us, and pray for this sacred Ceremony House to be reborn."

As Alex, Tate and Iná gathered, Belva began to chant in Navajo—

From outside, Alex heard an echo, the same chant, as if Belva's voice had grown deeper, wrapping around Turning Hawk land until it reached all the way to the pines.

CHAPTER 16
TATE

Camp Crazy Horse, late afternoon

THE "HAPPY" ceremony was ruined when Chi-Chi picked up a large black tobacco tie—a hex on the Ceremony House at Camp Crazy Horse. Grandma Florence, Veronica, and Chi-Chi packed up, and without a word, left immediately for home in Rosebud. Iná couldn't convince them to stay rather than drive alone on narrow gravel roads at night. Even she couldn't salvage Alex's reputation. Camp Crazy Horse and the Turning Hawk family were cursed.

"Get in, *Misun*," Iná insisted, as she went to her Midwife Express and switched to English as she eyed Tate. "Alex, bring the pickup you hide behind the shed in my backyard."

Oh-oh. No more Alex crawling in Tate's window. Old Hawk-Eye Iná saw everything, probably even that the spade was missing, which Alex had left at the cemetery.

Tate got in with Dr. Belva, who followed Iná and Alex in the Midwife Express, into the driveway of 44 Eagle Nest Housing, where they found the front door and kitchen door open.

"Who's in my house?" Iná ran up the kitchen steps. "Where are my midwives?"

Maybe the midwives had gotten a call. People came to get a midwife, or just to visit and eat. But how could they leave without the Midwife Express? Or was the call was a ruse to leave the house empty? But who would have gone to such trouble to get rid of the midwives?

Tate, and Dr. Belva followed Iná, but Alex had gone around to the front door to check that no one was in the basement.

The house had been ransacked, but by whom—an intruder or by Flossie's revenge? Pots and pans cluttered the floor of the kitchen. The living room rug pushed aside. Sofa pillows and chairs thrown helter-skelter. Dining table tossed on its side. Tate stumbled to her piano. Its dark wood was unscratched—a miracle! Then she rushed into her room. Blankets and clothes had been tossed or thrown on the floor, but the old cradleboard underneath the bed was safe.

Dr. Belva checked her belongings, then went outside and locked her car. Their affidavits were safe in the trunk.

One door was still locked from the inside. Tate called, "Grandma Agatha, are you okay?"

The last midwife unlocked her door and emerged, her clothes dusty. "You back at last!"

"Who was it?" demanded Iná.

"Closed window, locked door on noisy man."

"How many? What did they want?"

"He bang, bang, bang. Mad. I push bed against door and crawl under."

"Was he banging the piano?" Tate asked. As she played Middle C, a slow resistant muffled sound emerged. She raised the piano lid. Underneath, between the strings lay wisps of feathers, short-shafted black-and-white feathers. Had one of her piano kids in the Housing Circle come in and played a trick on her? She raised the piano lid high and propped it up with its stick. Reaching into the piano's belly, she pulled out as many feathers as she could that were caught among the metal strings, creating an eerie metallic discord of notes floating into the living room.

Iná ran into the room, grabbed one of the feathers and dropped it instantly. "Ai-yee," she cried. "Not eagle plumes. Them's owl feathers! Owl feathers—aren't they from Navajo country? Isn't Belva Navajo?"

Dr. Belva looked at the feathers. "Yes, they are owl feathers."

"Owl feathers—they come from Navajo country? Did you bring them with you?"

"Of course not."

"So you are Navajo. What do they mean?"

"In my land owl feathers are very precious, only kept by wise old women, healers and seers, who learn wisdom from each feather."

"This is Lakota land, not north, not south, but the Center of the Earth where the sacred Black Hills, Paha Sapa. We not scared of them. We bury owl feathers, not burn them with ashes to the winds, blowing them back to where they came."

Dr. Belva retreated to her room.

Iná yanked her broom out of the closet, swept the feathery pile onto the floor and stomped on them. "Don't touch! Owl brings death." She cried out, "*Misun!* Take 'em outside and burn 'em."

Tate knew that *Misun* meant: "my one and only son—who must do what I say—now."

Alex climbed up the basement stairs, looked at Tate holding the piano lid open, looked at Iná stomping the floor, and finally saw the pile of feathers beneath her feet.

"Death must leave my house," Iná said between gritted teeth.

Like a good son, he took her broom, swept them into a wastebasket, and carried the trampled feathers outside.

Tate reminded her mother-in-law that Dr. Belva couldn't have had anything to do with the Vision Cave dead baby threat. And just hours ago they were in the Ceremony House when Dr. Belva sang, and they all prayed together. Still, Tate worried that Iná might evict Dr. Belva and ruin their efforts to collect evidence for the lawsuit. She'd think of something to do.

After Alex buried the owl feathers, Iná went into action. First she locked all the doors. She hauled out the step ladder. Then she rummaged in the stairway closet for tools, took out a hammer and nailed each window to its sill, banging her way through the living room and bedrooms until all the windows were shut. Tate knew Iná wouldn't stop until she ran out of nails. Especially Tate's window.

Dr. Belva tried to reason with Iná when she nailed shut the windows in the guest room. Tate told her, "It's useless to resist, wait until the tornado is over."

Dr. Belva asked, "But don't you think someone is trying to give us a message to quit interviewing Lakota women?"

Tate replied, "It's not us. Otherwise, why the piano? Why not just slash tires or bash in the windshield of your rental car?"

Not finished, Iná re-checked all the doors, then went down in the basement to nail even the casement windows shut. Emerging with a hammer in one hand and nails in another, Iná said grimly, "I lock my doors, yet a *wanaghi* got in. So I nail that ghost out."

Now they all were locked in. Whew. Iná sat down at last.

Tate glanced at the lintel above the kitchen door, where years ago Alex had tucked a traditional string of red tobacco ties for protection. She couldn't see a hint of red there, but they were supposed to be hidden. She walked to the door and ran her hand above the lintel. Gone.

Gone over the side door as well. And over her bedroom door. She'd make more ties for both doors before Iná would notice. Or had she already noticed?

~~~

The Episcopal Church van pulled into their driveway and stopped. Doors banged open. The midwives had returned. They chattered at the news. "We've just come from a visit at a birth in Hisle." But they couldn't get in. Not only was the kitchen door locked, it was nailed shut.

Standing on the cement steps, they asked, "What's happened here?"

Alex pulled out two nails and unlocked the kitchen door.

As the midwives filled the kitchen, Iná confronted them. "You left the house unlocked, unprotected. Look downstairs, see if anything is missing."

"No, no, we took our healing baskets with us. A successful birth, a perfect baby girl."

"And they gave us a present to bring back for you, for keeping the Midwife House open." The midwives were so happy, but Iná barely accepted the woven shawl. She folded it and put it in her room. She was still angry. Unsettled. Afraid. The soul of her house had been desecrated, just like the Vision Cave.

Iná stomped down to the basement and brought up a gallon of gas. "They didn't get this," she said to everyone. "Now, *Misun,* you must bring Old Sam here."

But the roads toward Pine Ridge after midnight were dangerous. Tate handed Alex hot coffee in a mug with a lid, enough to keep him awake. Old Sam would give Alex more coffee for their return as well—for a daytime ceremony to purify both Midwife House and the Ceremony House at Camp Crazy Horse.

Dr. Belva went into her room and closed the door. Not another ceremony.

CHAPTER 17
ALEX

On the road to Calico, midnight

ALEX FOUND Clarence asleep in his pickup. Empty booze bottle. "Wake up, roadman, move over. Did you see anyone ransack my mother's house?"

"Didn't see nothing." He sucked at the empty bottle. "Heard stuff, though. Big cycle, hrmm-hrmm. Then later, a lotta crashing. Didn't go in, scared your mother'd blame me. It's safe in here, outta the way."

"If you're gonna ride with me, chuck that bottle, and the one underneath the seat."

Clarence nudged the full bottle under his boot. "Hey, I brought back your shovel."

Spade. But booze must have brought Clarence from the Episcopal Church cemetery to an Eagle Nest party house across the way. Whoever had ransacked the house was looking for something not there. Or just mad. They could have found Clarence first, asleep on the kitchen doorstep, and given him alcohol to get rid of him.

"Where we going?"

"Calico. Keep me company on the road."

Clarence opened his new bottle. "I knew yer old man, saw him at Eagle Butte Fair once, behind the stands, maybe ten years ago, maybe longer. I used to rodeo with 'im. He was the only one with an old-time Sioux saddle, pony beads and all. Always winning. Prayers and sweetgrass'll do it."

"Have you seen him since?" Alex asked. "Know where he went? West?"

"Nah. Been a long time ago. Where'n Calico you headed?"

"Old Sam's. He's supposed to come immediately to purify my mother's house."

"Lemme out here, then." Clarence jerked the door open, tossed out two empty bottles, and followed. "Don't like medicine men, they see right through you."

<p style="text-align:center">~~~</p>

In Calico, Alex knocked on the cabin door of Old Sam. He was often awake late in the night, like a night hawk. He told Old Sam what was happening with black ties, and now owl feathers. Iná insisted on a daytime ceremony immediately. After hot coffee, he started at the beginning: finding the dead baby in a black cradleboard in the Turning Hawk Vision Cave.

Old Sam said, "I heard otherwise that your reputation's been good. Healing a deaf child in the sweat lodge and telling the sex of an unborn child."

Either the Moccasin Telegraph had mangled its stories—or Old Sam was puffing them up to encourage him. Wanakcha hadn't been deaf, and wasn't a girl. Chi-Chi had grabbed a black tobacco tie. Maybe he hadn't yet heard the Rosebud gossip about another Turning Hawk baby.

"What else worrying you?" Old Sam poured another cup of black mud coffee.

"Worried about Tate, driving around all over the Res and asking older women whether they were sterilized or not, pushing them to sign papers for a lawsuit."

"It's May," Old Sam said, "time for *Hanblechia* out in the open on the Vision Hill, no longer hiding in the Vision Cave."

Alex sighed. He'd finished four years in the Turning Hawk Vision Cave to become a full-fledged *Wichasa Wakan,* a Lakota medicine man. Wasn't that enough? Now he'd be open to the elements, wind, rain, even snow in May sometimes, sun burning down like in the August Sundance. Coyotes; he'd even seen bear tracks once. *Wanaghi.* Ghosts. Where was Hawk, his night guardian? Not to be seen. Perhaps he'd fly in after dark.

When it was dawn, Alex drove Old Sam back to Eagle Nest. This was the fourth threat the Turning Hawk family had received: the dead baby at the vision pit, the empty baby's grave dug in their cemetery plot, the black tobacco ties nailed to the red hand of his cabin, and now owl feathers hidden in Tate's piano keys. He'd hidden from her that he'd found other black tobacco ties, and the work-boot footprint outside the Vision Cave.

CHAPTER 18
TATE

Camp Crazy Horse, late afternoon

THE "HAPPY" ceremony was ruined when Chi-Chi picked up a large black tobacco tie—a hex on the Ceremony House at Camp Crazy Horse. Grandma Florence, Veronica, and Chi-Chi packed up, and without a word, left immediately for home in Rosebud. Iná couldn't convince them to stay rather than drive alone on narrow gravel roads at night. Even she couldn't salvage Alex's reputation. Camp Crazy Horse and the Turning Hawk family were cursed.

"Get in, *Misun*," Iná insisted, as she went to her Midwife Express and switched to English as she eyed Tate. "Alex, bring the pickup you hid behind the shed in my backyard."

Oh-oh. No more Alex crawling in Tate's window. Old Hawk-Eye Iná saw everything, probably even that the spade was missing, which Alex had left at the cemetery.

Tate got in with Dr. Belva, who followed Iná and Alex in the Midwife Express, into the driveway of 44 Eagle Nest Housing, where they found the front door and kitchen door open. Hardly anyone locked their doors in Eagle Nest. But neighbors would know. Sooner or later, the Moccasin Telegraph would tell.

"Who's in my house?" Iná ran up the kitchen steps. "Where are my midwives?"

Maybe the midwives had gotten a call. People came to get a midwife, or just to visit and eat. But how could they leave without the Midwife Express? Or was the call was a ruse to leave the house empty? But who would have gone to such trouble to get rid of the midwives?

Tate, and Dr. Belva followed Iná, but Alex had gone around to the front door to check that no one was in the basement.

The house had been ransacked, but by whom—an intruder or by Flossie's revenge? Pots and pans cluttered the floor of the kitchen. The living room rug pushed aside. Sofa pillows and chairs thrown helter-skelter. Dining table tossed on its side. Tate stumbled to her piano. Its dark wood was unscratched—a miracle! Then she rushed into her room. Blankets and clothes had been tossed or thrown on the floor, but the old cradleboard underneath the bed was safe.

Meanwhile, Dr. Belva had checked her belongings, then went back outside and locked her car. Their affidavits were safe in the trunk.

One door was still locked from the inside. Tate called, "Grandma Agatha, are you okay?"

The last midwife unlocked her door and emerged, her clothes dusty. "You back at last!"

"Who was it?" demanded Iná.

"Closed window, locked door on noisy man."

"How many? What did they want?"

"He bang, bang, bang. Mad. I push bed against door and crawl under."

"Was he banging the piano?" Tate asked. As she played Middle C, a slow resistant muffled sound emerged. She raised the piano lid. Underneath, between the strings lay wisps of feathers, short-shafted black-and-white feathers. Had one of her piano kids in the Housing Circle come in and played a trick on her? She raised the piano lid high and propped it up with its stick. Reaching into the piano's belly, she pulled out as many feathers as she could that were caught among the metal strings, creating an eerie metallic discord of notes floating into the living room.

Iná ran into the room, grabbed one of the feathers and dropped it instantly. "Ai-yee," she cried. "Not eagle plumes. Them's owl feathers! Owl feathers—aren't they from Navajo country? Isn't Belva Navajo?"

Dr. Belva looked at the feathers. "Yes, they are owl feathers."

"Owl feathers—they come from Navajo country? Did you bring them with you?"

"Of course not."

"So you are Navajo. What do they mean?"

"In my land owl feathers are very precious, only kept by wise old women, healers and seers, who learn wisdom from each feather."

"This is Lakota land, not north, not south, but the Center of the Earth where the sacred Black Hills, Paha Sapa. We not scared of them. We bury owl feathers, not burn them with ashes to the winds, blowing them back to where they came."

Dr. Belva retreated to her room.

Iná yanked her broom out of the closet, swept the feathery pile onto the floor and stomped on them. "Don't touch! Owl brings death." She cried out, "*Misun!* Take 'em outside and burn 'em."

Tate knew that *Misun* meant: "my one and only son—who must do what I say—now."

Alex climbed up the basement stairs, looked at Tate holding the piano lid open, looked at Iná stomping the floor, and finally saw the pile of feathers beneath her feet.

"Death must leave my house," Iná said between gritted teeth.

Like a good son, he took her broom, swept them into a wastebasket, and carried the trampled feathers outside.

Tate reminded her mother-in-law that Dr. Belva couldn't have had anything to do with the Vision Cave dead baby threat. And just hours ago they were in the Ceremony House when Dr. Belva sang, and they all prayed together. Still, Tate worried that Iná might evict Dr. Belva and ruin their efforts to collect evidence for the lawsuit. She'd think of something to do.

After Alex buried the owl feathers, Iná went into action. First she locked all the doors. She hauled out the step ladder. Then she rummaged in the stairway closet for tools, took out a hammer and nailed each window to its sill, banging her way through the living room and bedrooms until all the windows were shut. Tate knew Iná wouldn't stop until she ran out of nails. Especially Tate's window.

Dr. Belva tried to reason with Iná when she nailed shut the windows in the guest room. Tate told her, "It's useless to resist, wait until the tornado is over."

Dr. Belva asked, "But don't you think someone is trying to give us a message to quit interviewing Lakota women?"

Tate replied, "It's not us. Otherwise, why the piano? Why not just slash tires or bash in the windshield of your rental car?"

Not finished, Iná re-checked all the doors, then went down in the basement to nail even the casement windows shut. Emerging with a hammer in one hand and nails in another, Iná said grimly, "I lock my doors, yet a *wanaghi* got in. So I nail that ghost out."

Now they all were locked in. Whew. Iná sat down at last.

Tate glanced at the lintel above the kitchen door, where years ago Alex had tucked a traditional string of red tobacco ties for protection. She couldn't see a hint of red there, but they were supposed to be hidden. She walked to the door and ran her hand above the lintel. Gone.

Gone over the side door as well. And over her bedroom door. She'd make more ties for both doors before Iná would notice. Or had she already noticed?

~~~

The Episcopal Church van pulled into their driveway and stopped. Doors banged open. The midwives had returned. They chattered at the news. "We've just come from a visit at a birth in Hisle." But they couldn't get in. Not only was the kitchen door locked, it was nailed shut.

Standing on the cement steps, they asked, "What's happened here?"

Alex pulled out two nails and unlocked the kitchen door.

As the midwives filled the kitchen, Iná confronted them. "You left the house unlocked, unprotected. Look downstairs, see if anything is missing."

"No, no, we took our healing baskets with us. A successful birth, a perfect baby girl."

"And they gave us a present to bring back for you, for keeping the Midwife House open." The midwives were so happy, but Iná barely accepted the woven shawl. She folded it and put it in her room. She was still angry. Unsettled. Afraid. The soul of her house had been desecrated, just like the Vision Cave.

Iná stomped down to the basement and brought up a gallon of gas. "They didn't get this," she said to everyone. "Now, *Misun,* you must bring Old Sam here."

But the roads toward Pine Ridge after midnight were dangerous. Tate handed Alex hot coffee in a mug with a lid, enough to keep him awake. Old Sam would give Alex more coffee for their return as well—for a daytime ceremony to purify both Midwife House and the Ceremony House at Camp Crazy Horse.

Dr. Belva went into her room and closed the door. Not another ceremony.

CHAPTER 19
ALEX

To the Vision Hill, late afternoon

IT WAS time for *Hanblechia,* to enter the vision quest to end the curse on Turning Hawks.

He saw his way clear. This time he'd stand on a promontory to face the wind and dark, as well as sun and heat. Old Sam had told him it was time.

Everyone at the camp prepared for Alex's *Hanblechia.* At the Midwife House, Tate and Iná made hundreds of tobacco ties to make a rolled-up ball of red for his "fence," or "gate," while outside in his pickup Alex made his own ties for his altar. Then he gathered dried sage and cedar to sit on, and filled his small fasting pipe with kinnick-kinnick.

He missed Tate. They'd had no chance to reconcile their harsh words after Chi-Chi's failed fortune-telling, and now the women were doing women's work, men doing men's work. Even though she wouldn't be allowed around his sweat or the all-night fire for those who kept watch during his fasting, just her presence would give him strength. She kept the camp warriors from fighting by teasing them, and unlike Mabel, who had left the camp, she got up early and cooked big meals for the work crew, pancakes and gravy, commodity beef stew, kabuk bread, and always, hot coffee steaming on the woodstove.

Meanwhile Old Sam rounded up the Camp Crazy Horse warriors to stake out a fasting site in the Badlands far from civilization. The warriors built a sweat lodge, fire pit, gathered wood, and heated rocks, ready for the evening ceremony. Then they came for Alex and brought him to the Vision Hill overlooking Redstone Basin, a place marking where Chief Big Foot in 1890 led his band in the December snows toward Wounded Knee.

That night he joined Old Sam and the AIM warriors for his fasting sweat. He ducked inside after Old Sam, alone with his teacher and the ancient rocks to steam and sing and pray.

Afterwards, he wrapped himself in the red blanket, carrying his small fasting pipe bound with sage. This time he took his own beaded lizard *chekpa ognake* with him on his vision quest and prayed with it, prayed for insight, for knowledge, to find a cure.

He followed Old Sam with the flashlight out to the ledge of the promontory of the Badlands shale facing north. He closed his eyes as Old Sam unrolled the ball of red tobacco ties on the ground and fenced him inside the Sacred Hoop. He held his small pipe aloft while Old Sam sang the lonesome *Hanblechia* cry for the Spirit People to come. As the song echoed in the Badlands arroyos below, a cold breeze carrying dry rock dust ruffled his damp hair, and in the distance, a shrill night hawk cry. As Old Sam returned to the sweat lodge fire to keep vigil night and day, Alex entered the Spirit World.

~~~

Alex was more determined than ever to find a real cure, not just making a joke, like with Wanakcha and Chi-Chi. This hexing would not be cured by herbs growing on the land, gopher power to dig in the earth. This was a much older curse, and only stone medicine would work, old fossils of teeth and bone and shell found only in the Badlands below him. He prayed for his Hawk power to fly out and above, see the teeth and bones and shells, and then with shrill "kree–kree," dive down and grab them with his talons, with his beak, and carry them back to his small fasting altar in front of his grandfather's Vision Cave.

Instead, during the first night Alex woke to a nightmare about Tate in peril, which kept him awake but drowsy. No vision came, only Tate's face bobbing up and down, as if she agreed she was driving too fast in a topsy-turvy world.

CHAPTER 20
TATE

On the road to Manderson and Oglala, morning

TATE HAD been told to stay away from Alex on the Vision Hill, not to distract him from his prayers. To make sure, Iná handed her an embroidered Medicine Wheel pillow in a carryall bag.

"Be sure to visit Auntie Violet in Manderdson first while you two drive around the Res."

That meant Iná hadn't gone to see her Auntie in weeks. She had an obligation to honor older relatives with a gift: stay an hour, stay to eat, even stay overnight because Res roads were dark and dangerous. Dr. Belva might understand: they'd have to leave Auntie Violet's before noon to drive further to Oglala, where they'd find AIM women more willing to be interviewed about private matters like sterilization or the shame of producing only one child, and they'd collect more affidavits.

This time Belva insisted on driving. She'd noticed that Tate had barely fit under the steering wheel. Even though Dr. Belva was used to city driving, not on the rough gravel roads. Instead, she kept a lookout for that big pickup that seemed to follow them wherever they went.

As Dr. Belva drove into Manderson to visit Iná's relative, Tate realized it would be a waste of time. Auntie Violet, like Iná, had only one child, and would sit polite and silent about a lawsuit, but ready to hear the newest Eagle Nest gossip.

Tate handed the carryall bag to Auntie Violet and watched her delight at the embroidered Medicine Wheel pillow. By mid-morning both Tate and Dr. Belva had listened patiently to advice about baby names, beaded lizard bags, and herbal cures. At last Aunt Violet rose, went to her cupboard, and handed each a clutch of *cheyaka* leaves for tea, which they accepted gracefully and rose to leave. "Harold," she said. "My dead husband's name. Time to pass it on."

They reached Oglala and parked in front of the double-wide College trailer, hoping to find older women students more willing to be interviewed. When they walked into the Director's office, a red-haired woman was on the phone, asking, demanding supplies. Tate could hear voices from a classroom at the other end of the trailer. It sounded similar to town meetings or oratory at the Old Treaty gatherings.

With a burst of laughter, the college door opened, and women of all ages rushed past to their cars in the parking lot. Tate noticed both full-bloods and half-breeds, women out to get an AA degree so they could be Teacher Aides at the BIA schools and Headstart, incorporating Lakota language and concepts in the classroom. Some had cut their hair short, even a buzz. Some wore dresses with stockings rolled to their knees. Others wore ragged jeans and cut-short t-shirts. Two were even pregnant. What a mixture. Some would talk to Dr. Belva.

Despite many boyfriends and a current legal husband, the Director had only one child. She took in foster kids. When she had her first delivery in Pine Ridge Hospital in 1961, she was put under totally and woke up later without knowing what had happened. When later she failed to conceive, she thought at first that her boyfriends were sterile, but later realized it was herself. Yes, she would sign a paper for her records to be released.

Fortunately, Tate didn't have to translate. Word had spread about the Denver lawsuit. So they collected over twenty signed affidavits.

~~~

On the way home Dr. Belva said, "I'd heard that Wounded Knee '73 held a secret Ghost Dance revival. Now I want to see the original place where the Ghost Dance was held."

Tate had never been to The Stronghold near Red Shirt Table at the far northwest part of Pine Ridge Reservation, where Wovoka's Ghost Dance had been held for many weeks in late 1890 before the U. S. Army slaughtered Big Foot's Band at Wounded Knee. But she'd heard the tales of *Oonakizin,* the sacred Table—a mesa jutting out into the Badlands. Wovoka, a Paiute weather doctor, so she'd heard, had a vision of Indians, both living and dead, dancing together in a circle to drive White settlers off Indian Treaty land forever.

Wovoka had said that Mother Earth would roll over herself by landslides, earthquakes, and tornadoes. And Alex had told her that once he'd been shown an old Ghost Dance shirt relic stitched with dried wild cucumber seeds and painted designs meant to repel bullets. One of his ancestors had believed that they could dance a New World into being. Now the site was nothing but hillocks of grass that overlooked western Badlands and U.S. Air Force Gunnery Range.

Even though it was getting late, with Tate navigating they found their way on a gravel road past Red Shirt Table. Unlike Bosque Redondo, where the Navajo were penned up inside canyons for weeks in the 1860s, the Stronghold was wide open to the elements, on the top of a mesa overlooking the Badlands. Like a long finger, or a skinny neck leading to a wide round head, it dropped down a thousand feet.

For the Ghost Dancers there was no protection from the elements, and no place to hide or run from the Army soldiers coming from Pine Ridge Agency to arrest them.

Tate was hungry, and her baby was kicking inside. Eighty miles to go. The sun had already set. Yet the trip was worth collecting more affidavits for the lawsuit. While Dr. Belva drove, Tate directed her toward the town of Interior, after which they could save miles by taking a short cut back to Eagle Nest called the Interior Cut-off, a narrow gravel road winding up through the Badlands.

In the twilight Tate peered at the entrance to an unmarked dirt road heading south out of the Badlands up onto the prairie. She urged Dr. Belva on. "Yes, this is the short cut," she insisted. "It'll save us an hour, and we don't have to go through the junction where everyone heads back from Interior Bar."

Dr. Belva headed uphill. "You sure?" she asked as the car rattled over gravel ruts. "It's like driving over corrugated roofing." She looked sideways at Tate. "You okay?"

Tate had forgotten that there were no guard rails on the gravel roads, only gravel berms. Tate shuddered in her seat as the car bumped uphill and dust rolled in the open windows. She coughed and rolled up her window while her baby bounced inside her. "It'll smooth out."

But it didn't smooth out. The ruts got worse and the road narrowed. Dr. Belva grumbled and shifted into low gear. As they climbed up further, the road curved and twisted. But it was the right road. Tate remembered the turns. On the passenger side, she looked down over the edge into the deep arroyos, shadows deepening from deep purple to black. She loved the rugged sharp angles of the Badlands, stark in the oncoming twilight.

A carload of drunks in a one-headlight car passed them, but Dr. Belva bravely hugged the cliff side of the road, and kept driving. They heard a horn blast "*ooga,ooga*," as if from an old jalopy, followed by shrieks and yells. Then the screech of brakes grating on gravel, and the jalopy disappeared downhill.

Whew. They were almost out of the Badlands. Tate stared out the windshield. Clouds of dust rose in front. As Dr. Belva slowed around a curve in the road, she yelled, "Watch out! Another car. More lights ahead!"

A jacked-up chrome-plated cowboy pickup with a rack of deer lights overhead turned a corner and fishtailed directly at them. The driver clung to the cliff side, forcing Belva to swerve toward the gravel berm at the far edge of the road. Then the pickup's high front bumpers hit the driver's side of the car, forcing Belva's rental car to spin off the road and down. Down into a gulley, rolling over. And over.

Crash, bang, bang.

Until the rental car stopped.

One last bang, then silence.

They were belted in. Upside down.

～～～

When Tate came to, woozy, surrounded by darkness, she felt a weight on her stomach. Not her baby but her seat belt holding her to the roof. No, to the floor if she weren't upside down, tightly belted still. So tight that her baby was kicking in protest. Alive! Safe inside. She prayed for her baby girl to stay alive. She took deep breaths even though her knees hurt.

The Mercedes had crumpled, landing on the left side with a loud crash, stopped by a boulder. Dr. Belva lay beneath her, half out of the windshield. It was hard to see her through the broken glass.

"Dr. Belva?" she cried. She reached downwards toward where Dr. Belva must be and touched something. Dr. Belva's left arm was twisted around the steering wheel, broken. Glass splinters shone on the back of her braided hair.

"Dr. Belva!" No answer.

Upside down, held in by the seat belt that was squashing her baby, she braced her legs against the dashboard. It was totally dark, only the instrument panel glowing. She held her belly with both hands to protect Baby Two Heart inside. Still a heartbeat—their two hearts must make it out of this disaster. If she could reach the glove compartment, if she had a knife to hack herself free—even with her teeth—

She cried for the Great Mystery to help her save her baby and herself.

CHAPTER 21

ALEX

On the Vision Hill, after midnight

ALEX TURNING Hawk felt his fasting pipe slipping from his hands. He'd dozed off in the middle of his *Hanblechia*, the sacred fasting for the coming Sundance and the birth of his baby. He reached in the darkness for his pipe, grasping the sage wrapped around it and held it tight to his chest. Had a hawk cry, his Hawk cry, "kree–kree"— awakened him? He listened. Some other cry echoed in the distance above, back at Camp Crazy Horse where Old Sam, his medicine man mentor, was keeping watch with his AIM warriors around the sweat lodge fire. Old Sam had taken him out to the Vision Hill during the night, and would keep watch over him until he had finished his fast.

He heard another cry, a screech, a scream piercing the darkness, echoing off the Badlands Wall, and footsteps running down the trail to the Vision Hill. Amid low mutterings he recognized his mother's high-pitched irate voice. She knew the customs: no one could interrupt a *Hanblechia*, since the person fasting had entered the Spirit World. Only Old Sam could come to check on him at dawn, and it wasn't dawn yet. Wrapped in his red blanket, he clutched the small pipe tighter and prayed to the Great Mystery for help. Only a disaster would bring her here.

He stood at the edge of the Badlands Wall facing north, looking out across the thirty-mile expanse, looking down into the deep arroyos and sharp escarpments.

Badlands below—

Vision Hill above—

Noises behind—

Flashlight beam in his painted face—

"*Misun,*" Iná cried. My son. "*Wana, taichu—*" She stepped over the sacred fence of tobacco ties protecting him, grabbed him by the arms, and yanked him upright. "Come!" she demanded, and then mumbled something about his wife, Tate.

Behind her Old Sam entered and pushed her aside. "*Hiya.*" No. But Old Sam had been unable to stop her. She'd always been a fast runner, always gotten her way.

Alex's fast had been broken. To stop Iná from assaulting a Medicine Man and old friend, he stepped between them and handed Old Sam his small fasting pipe in the ceremonial manner. Turning Hawk Honor was already broken. Then he took Iná's trembling hands and started down with her from the Vision Hill.

"Car wreck," she cried, dragging him down the trail by flashlight. "You have to be there to save my grandson." She led him past the AIM warriors sitting by the dying embers of the sweat lodge rocks still in the fire pit for the morning.

Back at the Midwife Express, Iná handed him jeans, shirt and boots, then the large Turning Hawk pipe resting across the dashboard. "I drive, you pray," she said. Her mouth closed tight. No explanation.

His eagle feather hanging above the dashboard of Midwife Express swayed as she turned sharply onto the gravel road.

This was not a good idea. It was still dark and Iná needed more than her sewing glasses. He was a better driver, even if he'd just been yanked out of the Spirit World.

She gripped the steering wheel as if by doing so, the car would go faster. She whipped up the gravel road to the gate and onto the paved highway. "Pine Ridge Hospital," she said, grinding her teeth. "*Wachekia.*" Pray.

Alex dressed on the way, braided his long hair, loose from fasting, with red ribbon and strips of mink to prepare for the hospital confrontation. He braced his knees against the dashboard and held the family pipe securely in his arms. He sang his prayer songs, one after another, knowing she wouldn't interrupt him. She'd yelled herself out back at the camp, but now she was silent. All her energy was in the gas pedal. She was heading toward hell, the Pine Ridge Indian Hospital, which as a midwife she'd sworn never to enter.

He prayed for pregnant Tate, he prayed for his unborn baby. Then he prayed for the car to stay on the road, for the engine not to burn out, for any horses to get off the road, all the trivial things, so the Great Mystery would keep death away.

As they neared Pine Ridge Village, Iná slowed slightly. Her energy had run down; her mouth opened and gossip poured out. Alex wished she'd kept silent because his mother had listened to the rumors about a Turning Hawk baby in the Pine Ridge Morgue.

He stopped her. "Think about Tate and Belva in the car wreck, pray for your unborn grandson. I know this baby is mine. Spirit People told me."

"Hmmf. You think I not been praying, step on the gas pedal to race on the road?" She pulled into the hospital parking lot and sat upright.

All that *inachni-inachni* rush to arrive, and now his mother sat stiff-bodied in the parking lot. He touched Iná's shoulder with the big pipe to remind her of the reason they were here. Perhaps she resisted entering the hospital she feared and distrusted. At last she reached behind her for her satchel, full of salves and herbs, and her diamond willow cane. Her protection. She got out and leaned on it, as if weak and frail. If they didn't let her in to see her daughter-in-law, he knew she'd rap the cane loudly on the intake desk and threaten the nursing staff.

CHAPTER 22
TATE

Pine Ridge Hospital, Tate's Room, after midnight

SCRAPING NOISES from an open door—squeaking wheels, crash of glass woke her. Tate moaned. Shaking. The bed was shaking her shoulder. She turned her head and sank back into blankness. Her name. Someone calling her. Holding her hand. With a great effort, she opened her eyes. The room was shadowy, but a white hospital uniform bent over her. A nurse, a doctor? A face shimmered above her, fading in and out. A *wanaghi*, a ghost. She blinked to shake off her dizziness. It was holding her hand. Big and warm. She clutched the hand so the face wouldn't vanish. Her mouth was dry, but she choked out, "Alex?"

No reply. She turned her head away. Ghosts didn't talk. A red headband floated above the face. Not Alex. An AIM guy from Camp Crazy Horse, one with long black braids? Too tall, taller even than Belva. Dark eyes full of tears, a face very sad, as if from the grave. She breathed in incense, not sage or sweetgrass, something sweet and heavy hovering over her. What was it?

"Where's Alex? I want him."

"Tate, he's on his way."

She moaned. A ghost had called her name. Was she dead? It wasn't Alex's hand that held hers, so she reached down to let go. But her hand—it was her hand—was tied to the bed, and an IV connected to a thin tube hanging overhead. "Alex must have given you my name, and sent you from the Spirit World?"

A deep quiet voice said, "You were in a car wreck."

No, she was in a bed in a white room, but now she no longer ached everywhere.

"In the Badlands. The seat belt saved you. EMTs cut you loose and brought you here."

She wanted his face to go away, so she closed her eyes. "Not the hospital. I want the midwives—" She ran out of breath. An ache across her ribs, ache between her thighs. She grabbed her belly with her free hand. Flabby. Empty. "My baby's gone!" Tears filled her eyes. "Is my baby dead, too?"

The man shook his head and smiled. "Your baby's fine. The seat belt saved you both."

Frantic, she tried to sit up. "Where's my baby?"

A pillow was pushed behind her back. "In the nursery, down the hall."

"Can you bring her to me? I want to see her—oh, you're a ghost." She fumbled one-handed to loosen the knotted cloth strip. "Wait. Is Dr. Belva in the next room?"

The ghost hesitated. "Dr. Belva? The Indian lawyer? She's—the ghost took a breath—she's in a different ward than maternity."

So Dr. Belva was okay. But the affidavits. "Did you find Belva's briefcase?"

"I'll check the wreck site again and bring it to you," the ghost man said, fading into the white wall, leaving behind—yes, the sweetness of honey.

CHAPTER 23
ALEX

Pine Ridge Hospital, after midnight

WHILE ALEX checked in at the Admissions Desk to find Tate's status, Iná slipped behind him, carrying his unfinished cradleboard, tapping her diamond willow cane, and disappeared.

Turning around, he saw her at the elevator. How did she know Tate was upstairs? He was sure she'd never been in an elevator before. But neither had he.

She pressed each button with her cane, and the door slid open.

"Wait," he called, and ran after her before the night attendant could stop him.

Inside, as the door closed, she said, "First we go Down, then Up! Before they catch us."

What was this, his mother playing games? With Tate upstairs terribly wounded from the car crash, maybe even dying?

The elevator jerked and creaked as it descended. He didn't want to go Down because he'd already been down in the Morgue.

"See if gossip is true," she said, pounding her cane. "Turning Hawk baby in basement."

When the door opened, he blocked it. "You don't want to see. We came here for Tate."

Upstairs in the deserted maternity ward they found a closed door, knocked, and went in. He silently closed the door behind them. In the dim light Alex saw a mound of sheets in a hospital bed, a hand taped to the railing. He slid to the side of the bed and touched the small plain wedding ring. His Tate. He stroked her tied hand. As he pulled the sheets away, he brushed the long black hair from her face and kissed her. She murmured and turned away. Then he saw her bruised face and closed eyes, heard her shallow breathing in drugged sleep.

Iná stood beside him, pulled the covers down further, and gently caressed Tate's belly. Using her flashlight, she examined the area. Bandaged, soft but flat. "No baby in belly! Baby upside-down got strangled dead? "Ay-iee—" she cried. "Or cut her open and pull out live baby? Where's my grandson?"

Tate stirred. "A nurse took my baby away," she mumbled and fell back asleep.

Alex could hardly breathe at the possibilities. Blood on the sheets. Did his son die in the car wreck? Would Tate die? Would his son live?

Iná cried, "Crime to separate baby from mother instead of laying it by mother to nurse!" She opened her satchel full of midwives' herbs and salves and coated Tate's body with a thick pungent salve. "*Misun,*" Iná said, "don't give up. We purify this room, protect your wife. Now let her sleep while we find my grandson."

While he sat beside Tate as he prayed and made tobacco ties to tuck out of sight over the hospital door, Iná wrapped their cradleboard in an extra sheet and tucked it far under the bed. Together they smoked the room with sage and cedar, then opened a window a few inches to let the Great Mystery in.

Iná sniffed. "They gave her drugs to make her look like dead? But I smell honey."

"Where is the nursery?" Iná raced down the hallway and turned the corner. He barely caught up with her before she reached the glass-walled room. She stood transfixed, as if the rows of bassinettes had frozen her to the floor. "*Shicha!*" Bad.

He looked through the glass windows at the rows of bassinettes. How odd to see the small newborns wrapped in blankets, each in its own isolated box, constant light overhead, like cocoons in a beehive, crying because they are all alone. How could they thrive? No wonder they were crying, wrinkling up their faces, kicking off their blankets and waving their fists in the air. They should be next to their mothers, feeling the warmth of the mother's body, the love and joy. The mother holding the tiny hand, stroking each tiny finger, amazing miracle, perfect skin and eyes and curved mouth.

White doctors and nurses didn't know that a part of every Lakota's soul, called *tun,* lives forever, and that the souls of those gone on returned from the sky to fill the soul of a newborn baby. Without this *tun* the baby could not live. Even the way to announce a birth was thus: "A baby traveler has arrived."

Standing at the nursery window, he could feel the weak *tun* of several of the babies, some born prematurely without a *tun*. "Iná, they won't let you in there."

"Hoh!" she replied, pulling the door open and rushing in. "Where is my grandson?" she demanded of the nurse feeding a baby in her arms.

"You aren't allowed in here, Grandmother," the Lakota nurse replied. "If you go back outside and wait at the window, I'll bring him close to show you."

Iná swept her arms around the room. "Feeding it cow's milk, bred to stupidity, not letting it nurse at the breast! I hear about such things, but to see it with my own eyes—ayeee!"

The nurse shrugged. "Who's the mother and I'll bring her baby after I finish here."

Alex intervened. "It's the Turning Hawk baby."

"Oh, yes." The other nurse turned. "We've already had trouble with that one."

"Trouble? If he not alive—" Iná threatened.

"Of course he's alive. No germs. We have preemies here." The nurse advanced. "Out! We who work here must wear sterile gowns, gloves and masks. We can't allow contamination."

Iná began keening, weeping. "Crime, keeping babies away from their mothers, both die of loneliness. A marketplace and no one around."

Alex took his mother by the elbow and led her out of the room.

The nurse closed and locked the door. "Sir, I'll bring your baby to the window."

Iná turned around. Her face lit up, her eyes sparkled. She waved her fingers at the wide-eyed baby. "A boy! We must bring him to Tate. But first—"

He guessed what she was after: the *tun,* her grandson's birth cord.

"Must be on same floor," said Iná. "What you call it, Delivery Room. Been in one once, so I can sniff it out here, if not too late." She poked into doors until she found it.

Alex followed her as she found the Delivery Room, now deserted. He locked the door and looked around. No need to sniff; the air reeked of blood and alcohol. Tables overturned. Bloody sheets on the floor. A pallet with metal contraptions for feet overhead. Metal tongs in the sink. Was this where Tate had been taken?

Iná reached into a closet and brought out coats, pants, aprons, socks. "First we put on what they call the 'Whites.' White booties over shoes, white pants, white doctor coat, small cap. I put on nurse dress, white cap. Cover hair. You guard door. I find *chekpa ognake.*"

Though he pulled the 'whites' over his clothes and boots, he wouldn't fool anyone.

As Iná in her white dress and apron inspected him, she tucked his long braid beneath a white cap. "Now you look like a doctor. If someone knock, talk like a doctor. Otherwise, walk around hospital, find Tate's birth doctor. We must see that foreign doctor, find how he pulled my grandson out."

Leaning against the locked door, he watched what he had never seen before. His midwife mother rummaged in the wastebaskets until she found a wrinkled birth cord and sniffed it.

"Don't look," she said, "make men sick."

He pretended to turn away. Was this inside Tate all these months?

"Sometimes it twist like a telephone cord," she said. "Can't take whole, has to dry." After washing the birth cord in the sink, she cut off a piece, wrapped it in a bandage, put it in her beaded lizard bag, the one she'd made for a boy, and stuffed it all into her bulky satchel. "Now this belongs to my grandson."

His mother was amazing.

~~~

Behind him Alex heard a key turn in the lock. Not the young foreign doctor on a three-year stint. Instead, he faced a chunky white-haired man wearing a white coat, too, which hung loose, revealing cowboy shirt, belt and leather boots. No name tag on the pocket. Must be retired.

Dr. White Hair honed in on him. "You ignorant Morgue attendant, what are you doing up here, trying to play doctor?" He pushed past Alex toward Iná. "And you old nurse, why are you rummaging in the bloody trash? Drugs? I'll have you both fired!"

Turning around, Iná revealed her authoritative 'fierce face.' "Who are you?" she asked and squinted. "Don't I know you, Doctor White Hair?" In Lakota she said, "Do I recall him from somewhere? He wears rings. Most doctors take them off." Then, slipping a loose stethoscope under her apron, she tossed her full satchel to Alex and headed for the door.

Alex caught her satchel deftly and saw her theft. How had Iná known he'd wanted to make his own stethoscope, but without metal? He dodged Dr. White Hair and fled with Iná to the elevator and down to the first floor near the hospital entrance.

After their escape, Alex, still wearing 'whites,' went off to find the young foreign doctor in the middle of the night, but there was no one around, only an ambulance driver and two nurses who'd birthed his and Tate's baby, heading back to the dorm to sleep. It was strange and eerie—a whole hospital asleep, just occasional moans, clank of metal gurneys, and smells so antiseptic you could hardly breathe. He walked out to pray and connect with the earth—a lonely grassy plot with one tree.

CHAPTER 24
TATE

Pine Ridge Hospital, Tate's Room, before dawn

DRUGGED, TATE woke up from a heavy dream and looked at the ceiling. A white room, blinding overhead white lights. So bright, she must be alive, lying in a bed with white sheets tucked in with a white flannel blanket. A bed with metal railings. She was in a hospital, in Pine Ridge, in a white room. Outside were noises—coughing, squeaking wheels, rattle of glass.

She had to get up. Her arm wouldn't move. Her hand was stuck to the bedrail with a roll of white gauze taped down to the back of her hand by a band-aid. Yet she felt nothing. A skinny tube ran from her hand to an upside-down plastic bag hooked overhead. Transparent poison dripped from the bag into her tied-down hand. Dizzy, she shut her eyes to make the sudden pain go away. But she still felt it, the ache deep in her gut, between her legs, oh yes—the pain, the endless surges of pain, when she wanted to get up and run away, down the hall, out the corridor, into the outside under a tree or at least lie on the grass, anything but lie upside down with her legs spread. Pregnant, the baby wanting out, kicking and elbowing its way.

When she opened her eyes she remembered the accident. It came back in a rush: the rack of deer-hunting headlights blinding Dr. Belva, the crash, then rolling over and over, then upside down—the long bumpy drive while in labor. No one had told her the cramps would wrack the breath out of her. Jerry the ambulance driver, speeding like a demon, swerving at all the unbanked curves on old Res roads. Then the hospital at night, empty, making her sit down on a wheelchair instead of letting her walk in to the labor room. Lying down and sweating, crying out and cursing, when she wanted to get up and pace back and forth until she collapsed or died.

She'd known to stay away from the Indian Public Health Hospital in Pine Ridge. Iná had filled her with stories of botched operations and wrong diagnoses, so she'd decided to let the midwives in Eagle Nest birth her baby.

With her free hand she felt her belly. The pain in her belly—her belly was almost flat. No baby inside. Where was Baby Two Heart!

Some doctor must have pulled her baby out. Taken from her belly, bruised and dead? Strangled by the seat belt? Or half-alive and maimed for life? Was that why they didn't bring Baby Two Heart to her? She needed to hold her baby to know she was alive.

Beside her was a bottle of water and glass with a straw in it. Oh—Where was her baby? Did she have a boy or a girl? Healthy and perfect, or not? Why hadn't anyone told her? Why couldn't she remember seeing it? "Halloo, anyone there?" she called.

No answer. With her free hand Tate groped for a call button and pressed it over and over. Vague noises outside the room, in the hallway—more rattle and squeak of cart wheels, thumps, muffled cries. Where was Alex? The doctor? A nurse? How could they leave her alone? She'd find her baby herself.

With a surge of energy, she sat up and almost fainted from the pain in her stomach. Her arm was tied to the bedrail with an IV in her wrist.

With her free hand she yanked the gauze loose from the bedrail to release her numb hand. As she started to rip off the tape, she stopped. She'd need a cane to walk. Nothing in the room to lean on. Only the sturdy IV stand with its four little wheels. So she left the IV in.

Her belly hurt. Her back hurt. When she took a deep breath, her ribs hurt. She pushed off the covers and forced her legs to swing over the side of the bed. Then she grabbed the IV stand and slid off the bed unsteadily onto the cold floor. She grabbed hold of the cabinet by the bed to steady herself as she shuffled toward the door, dragging the IV stand with one hand and reaching for the door knob with the other. The long corridor was empty. But which way led to the nursery? She sniffed for talcum powder and wet diapers, listened for wailing babies, but heard only a squeaking cart.

She leaned out. In the distance, she saw a nurse's aide dressed in a pink uniform, wheeling a bassinette. She pressed her forehead to shake off dizziness and followed. Before she could turn the corner, the nurse's aide grabbed her from behind and forced her to turn around.

"What are you doing out of bed?" You're not supposed to be up yet."

"I want to see my baby!"

"Which room?"

"I don't know which room is the nursery, that's why I must find it."

"No, which room are you in?"

"Back there." When the nurse looked puzzled, Tate added, "Turning Hawk room."

"Oh, the Turning Hawk baby. I'm sorry, but—"

Tate pulled away from her, leaving the nurse holding the blanket. "I want my baby!"

She stumbled down the other corridor toward the noise of babies crying. She stopped before a glassed-in room full of a dozen bassinettes in two rows. A few babies were all glassed in and tied to IVs, like hers, but had breathing tubes. She pushed open the door.

A young nurse's aide dressed in pink put down the swaddled baby she was holding and came toward Tate. "Oops! You can't come in here. This is a sterile area. I'm sorry."

Tate backed up. "I just want to see my baby—"

"Yes, you can see your baby. Now, please back up and wait outside by the windows."

Tate let the aide ease her out the door. At last someone was listening to her, someone who was kind. Before long the aide came out with a blue and white striped bathrobe and put it around her. "You need to keep warm."

"I don't even know if it's a boy or a girl, and my husband's not here—"

"What name? I'll go see."

"Turning Hawk."

Tate leaned against the glass windows and pressed her forehead to see. Inside, the night aide went up and down the row.

At last she came out and said, "Are you sure? I don't see any Turning Hawk name, but the baby might not be back yet."

Blackness surrounded her. All those babies, and hers not there. Her baby was dead? No, she would have felt it. But if her baby wasn't right, couldn't breathe, or had some terrible deformity—maybe still in a recovery room from a traumatic birth. She pressed harder on the glass, as if by doing so she could see deeper into the room, and her baby would be there amid all the others. Tate grabbed the night aide's arm and asked, "Where is the operating room?"

The aide shook Tate's arm loose. "Let's go back to the nursing station. The head nurse will know." She turned Tate and the IV stand around, away from the windows, and walked her toward the nursing station at the far end of the hall. "They'll be able to tell you what's going on."

When they arrived at the nursing station, Tate leaned against the desk and pounded with her free hand. "My baby's not in the nursery. Where is she?"

Ignoring her, the head nurse rose from her seat like a solid and forbidding white stone statue. The statue moved swiftly around the desk, dodged the IV stand and shook the young aide. A deep smoker's voice emerged, filled with fury and authority. "What are you doing outside the nursery? What is it this time?"

Tate stood face to face with the white-haired statue. "My baby's missing. I demand to know where you're keeping her!"

"And you are?"

Tate felt a laser beam inspecting her: dark tousled hair, dark Indian face, her bare feet and bruised knees below the blue-and-white striped bathrobe the young aide had given her, then at the IV in her arm. She kept her voice steady and emphasized her native name: "Tate Turning Hawk. My newborn baby is missing. My husband Alex Turning Hawk from Eagle Nest, South Dakota, will arrive soon to file a complaint against this hospital."

The young aide shuddered, hung onto the IV stand, and began to sob.

The head nurse's laser-beam eyes flipped over to the aide and zapped her, then switched back to Tate. The deep smoky voice turned oily. "Now, Mrs. Turning Hawk, everything is fine. Your baby's being weighed and checked out by the doctor."

A White lie. Nothing was fine.

The white statue gripped Tate's free arm and stared at the white tiled floor behind her. "Look, you're bleeding. Let's get you back to bed."

Tate turned around. Behind her was a spotty trail of blood everywhere she'd been. She felt woozy for a moment, too weak to resist. With a nurse and aide at each elbow, she was dragged back to her room and put in bed. "I want Alex!" she cried.

The white statue ordered the terrified aide to raise the bedrails and lock them while she slid the IV stand into place and adjusted the drip bag. The same deep oily voice said, "We'll bring your baby to you, as soon as feeding time is over and nursery staff will have more time."

"I want my baby now! Can't you even tell me pink or blue?"

The lights went out. The door clicked shut.

After they left, Tate climbed over the rails, pulled the IV needle out, and found her bloody maternity clothes in the closet and put them on. No shoes. She put on the hospital's paper slippers and headed for the door.

She had to get out of here. Search the hospital top to bottom for Baby Two Heart. She'd open the door carefully to see if the corridor was empty, and sneak out. Still late at night. She turned the handle. It didn't budge.

She pounded on the door.

Screamed for help.

Couldn't catch her breath.

Scratched at the walls until her fingers bled.

CHAPTER 25
ALEX

Pine Ridge Hospital Nursery, before dawn

HE JOINED Iná on the way to the nursery. She'd decided that the *checkpa ognake* needed to be with their baby rather than tied to the new cradleboard.

Had they moved the baby they'd seen before? How could he tell which one was his? He stared through the glass at the boxes, one by one, feeling nothing, no heat, no connection. He felt empty—like the child who had chosen neither awl nor bow and arrows. How strange to feel no connection to his son when he could feel such a strong connection with his eagle feather. He had the feeling that his son wasn't there.

Alex said quietly, "Iná, that baby we looked at before isn't ours. Look closely."

Iná leaned against the glass. "Eh? It's a boy, *iteshni*? We already saw him. Just needs to be with his *checkpa ognake!*"

He disagreed. "It's a replacement. Our baby has disappeared."

"Hah!" said Iná. "How do you know?" She yanked at the nursery door, but this time it was locked. She rat-a-tatted on the glass.

"Nurse, I need to put something with my grandson you showed us earlier."

The young night aide looked frightened. "You can't come in. They said so."

Alex stood behind Iná . "Who said so?" He pointed to the last bassinette in the boys' row. "Look! Can't you see this one's empty?"

"Oh. A doctor in scrubs took him down to x-ray." She cringed. "To make sure."

Make sure of what? An X-ray at night? She was lying. No one does X-rays at 3am. "Who took the Turning Hawk baby?" he demanded.

She cringed. "My cousin. She said it was hers."

"Who's your cousin?" He already knew. Crazy Shuta. The dark green pickup in the parking lot. Ina was right, Shuta'd come back.

"*Iteshni.*" Told you so. Iná picked up her satchel containing the *checkpa ognake.* "I find Boss Nurse, pull Fire Alarm to wake doctor. You bring back my grandson."

He still had the keys to the Midwife Express. He prayed that it had enough power to rescue his son from Black Eyes Camp. And enough gas.

Outside, the dark green pickup in the parking lot was gone. In its place was an old battered black pickup with a well-used stock rack. Inside was the man he'd seen earlier, a Navajo Haatali named Ben, the brother of Belva, the Denver lawyer. What was he doing here in the hospital parking lot in the middle of the night? Had he been shadowing Tate and Belva, seen the accident, and followed to make sure both women were okay? Had he seen Shuta leave with his baby? Why had he parked in her empty spot? Had Ben been waiting for him with news?

He pulled beside Ben's pickup. The windows were shut, the engine off. Inside, Ben was slumped over, crying. Moaning. Singing. A traditional mourn ritual. He waited until Ben noticed him and rolled down the window.

"Tate will recover," Ben muttered, "but my twin sister has left this world."

Belva the Denver lawyer, dead? A great loss. Alex reached in and put his hand against Ben's chest. "*Kolá*, we will mourn with you."

"Not yet," Ben said. "When I came out of the Morgue I saw a woman running with a baby in her arms and driving away from this spot. I believe it was your son. Go after him!"

CHAPTER 26
TATE

Pine Ridge Hospital, Tate's Room, before dawn

HALF-AWAKE, TATE heard click-clicking. She smelled honey again, or was it bee pollen? Had the ghost man come again through the white wall, bringing a new sweetness? No, this time he'd come through the locked door. He carried a battered black briefcase, but when he saw her lying on the floor, he grabbed a chair and braced it against the door so no one could enter. She felt him pick her up off the floor, carry her to bed and tuck her in. Then he hid the briefcase behind the cradleboard under the bed.

"That's Dr. Belva's briefcase!" she cried. "You must have rescued all our affidavits! But how could you find it still in the wreck? Didn't the car burn up?"

"Not at first," he said. "I know how important it was to Belva."

"Oh, Ghost Man, do you know Dr. Belva?"

He smiled. "How did you get on the floor?"

"They locked me in but I had to get out to find my baby." Now she wasn't alarmed; instead, she felt protected, as if Alex on the Vision Hill had sent this Ghost Man from the fasting place in the Spirit World.

"No, don't try to get up." he said. He leaned over and laid his hands over the backs of hers, large fingers longer than hers. He lifted both pairs of hands onto her belly and hummed. She felt the power surge through his-then-her own palms, then into her body. Like a tuning fork or the low strings on a piano. Sometimes when she played, her fingers vibrated as their two palms did now. Her body tingled as they laid their hands on her bruised knees, scraped arms, her chest, her head. She was being healed. She asked, "Ghost Man, who are you, really?"

"I come from far, far away." He sang what seemed like a faraway song, releasing her hands and waving his, smudging the room with the honey fragrance.

It made her relax. "You've come to find my baby."

"Your baby is in the nursery," he said.

"Did you see her? Is Alex there? Can't you tell me more?"

"It's now I need *your* help."

She felt clear-headed and ready. Enough to help a ghost man. Why not?

He handed her a glass of water and a straw. "Rest, clear your head and talk to me. I need you to remember, moment by moment, what happened when you were on that gravel road out of Interior. Now, while the images in your brain are fresh."

She felt so mellow. Of course she'd help this ghost man. She lay back down and wiped her eyes. She didn't want to remember, but how could she forget the nightmare-like images, the screeches of metal on rock. "I can't think straight."

"Thank you. Rest your head and relax. Close your eyes."

She entered the dark world inside her eyelids and listened to his soft humming.

"You were driving up the back road from Interior."

His voice was deep and soothing. She nodded. They had collected so many affidavits at Oglala, she and Dr. Belva were going to celebrate.

He started the memory for her. "It was dark, but it hadn't rained. The gravel road was dry. You flipped on the brights."

"Mnnnh," she said. "Dr. Belva drove because I got too big to fit behind the wheel."

"Good. You are on the passenger side. Seat-belted in."

She remembered how tightly it fit. Then Dr. Belva's briefcase landed on her swollen ankles. As her memory sharpened, Tate shifted her legs.

"You are about halfway up from the Badlands, almost to the turn-off. A big truck comes around the curve towards you." He paused. "What's it look like?"

"First, the 'ooga-ooga' car full of drunks shrieking and yelling, but they missed us."

"After that, a big truck—"

"Pickup. Dark, hard to see," Tate said. Then there it was, looming before her eyelids. Instinctively she raised her arms to brace herself. "Big and wide. And high."

"Is it jacked up?"

"Big fat tires."

"Dual tires?"

She squinted. "Yeah, the kind of pickup that pulls a horse trailer."

"Horse rack?"

"No, more like a big camper top."

"Color? Make?"

She squirmed. "It's getting closer, hogging the road. Belva's yelling. Turning to hug the cliffside." Ahead was the layered rock cliff. They bounced off and swerved toward the overhang and… nothing—until she felt his soft honey-smooth hand stroking her forehead.

"Stay with me." the ghost man said. "The truck stops in the middle of the road."

She opened her eyes, wanting to grab his hand to make sure he wouldn't fade into the wall again. "No. It doesn't stop. It comes right at us. The big lights overhead blind us."

"A rack of strobe lights for poaching deer."

"Yeah, four haloes, so I can't see into the cab."

"Look down at the bumper. No license plate. Something in its place—a dealer's name?"

"More like a spider, legs sprawled out."

"Color?"

"Red, straight lines. Maybe a flag."

Silence.

Surrounded by the sweet fragrance.

"But when can I see my baby?" she asked.

Tate reached to grip his hand, but the room was dark—and empty again.

CHAPTER 27
ALEX

On the road to Black Eyes Camp, before dawn

ALEX KNEW where Shuta's family lived. Past the shot-up gate, into the open yard. Lester's dark green pickup was there, parked by her family's BIA house. Indian rock throbbed through the windows. Party time. He would wait until they ran out of booze. He parked the Midwife Express between the summer cook shack and an old wagon used for target practice so he could watch the front door unseen.

When the music stopped, he watched the family come busting out, led by Sonny, who stumbled and climbed in the pickup's driver side. The rest piled in the front and back as Sonny revved the engine and drove off.

Alex took his pipe bag from the dash and walked quietly up into the pines where he expected Shuta to be holed up in her family's old log cabin, once used for ceremonies long ago. He opened its door silently and stood there. Inside the small cabin was dark and hot, and smelled of burned beans and spoiled meat. In the gloom he saw Shuta sitting on a cot in the corner dressed in a black t-shirt and pants, her hair shorn to the roots, ashes on her face, her arms and legs slashed and scabbed, as if still in mourn. She rocked a crying baby in her arms, crooning to him in Lakota. His son.

Alex's soul reached out to him—I'm here! He wanted to tear his son from her arms, the thief, but he controlled his impulse, and calmly asked, "*Tokiya he?*"

She looked up and answered him in Lakota. "What're you doing here?"

"How are you, Shuta? I haven't seen you since you left Eagle Nest."

She slid back further on the cot, hiding the baby in her arms. "How'd you get past the house below? Where's Sonny? You came alone? Why are you here?"

"I've come for my son." He pointed to the baby.

She held him even tighter, and covered his face. "This baby is mine."

"You stole him from the hospital." He moved closer.

"No way. My baby's a Brave Heart."

"See the words on the blanket? Indian Public Health."

"So? I used to work there. But I gave birth to him right here." She reached under the pillow and whipped out a bloody rag from under the denim quilt. "I'm still bleeding, see?"

The rag was wrapped around a sheath knife, glinting in the darkness. No other knife like it: his grandpa's hawk knife, made for art and beauty, not death and destruction. Once it had been his. No other knife cut so cleanly, balanced so perfectly in his hands. When he'd whittled or carved, it became a hawk's talon. Without it, he might have forgotten his grandpa's presence. Last year he'd given it to a young AIM warrior who needed protection. Then it was stolen, just as Shuta'd stolen his son.

Let her keep the knife, he needed his son alive. She was deranged, lying. He edged closer. "May I see him? I could bless him with an eagle feather."

"No! Get away. He's mine." She backed away from him, knife in hand in front of his son.

"Look at him, Shuta. See his hawk nose, even as a baby, he's a Turning Hawk."

"No, you stupid blind idiot. He's not! He's my brother's baby! He told me he got your wife pregnant while you were gone." She hugged the bundle tighter. "So he's mine now, and I'm going to raise my nephew right, to be a warrior not a crazy *Pejuta Wichasa* like you."

She'd never believe that her brother had lied, just to be macho, just to 'count coup' on himself, a Medicine Man. "You're in mourn," he said softly.

"Sure!" She spat out the words. "I lost everything, my baby, my brother, my husband. So I cut myself, traditional way." She stared at him defiantly.

They'd all lost a lot, but Shuta more than most: during an AIM-goon shootout, she miscarried; a rogue FBI sniper killed her older brother-protector, and her husband jumped bail and left her to go into hiding.

"My brother told me to take his son, my nephew," she emphasized the Lakota word, *tunshka*, "and raise him right."

"You're in mourn. In pain." He took a step closer.

She raised the knife. Her face turned fierce. "Stay back, stay away from me! I'll cut him rather than let you have him!"

By the time he could grab for his grandpa's knife, she'd kill his son. He knelt down before her, praying that his grandpa's hawk knife would melt in her hands.

He hesitated, struggled with his thoughts. If he didn't return with his son, Iná would go on the warpath again, and Tate would call him a coward. He prayed silently to the Great Mystery for inner strength. At last he found the words. "Shuta, I don't want him killed. You keep him."

"I don't believe you." She glared at him. She still held the knife, now at his son's throat.

Slowly he reached behind him, pulled his Sacred Pipe from its bag, and held it in his hands outstretched before her. Its power flowed into his arms and chest, reaching his heart. Its solid stone bowl and the warm cedar stem gave him strength. The smell of dry sage and moist kinnick-kinnick took him back to the Sacred Sundance Tree of Life. In that moment he turned the care of his son over to *Tunkashila*, the Great Mystery. "Rather than let him be killed, I give him to you to keep him alive."

Shuta stared at him. "People lie on the Pipe."

"I've given my life to the Sacred Pipe. I could never misuse it, even to save my son." He rested the Pipe in his lap and reached into his bag again. "You're in pain. Let me put some herb salve on your arms."

"You're alone? No cops? No doctors?" She looked around warily.

He knelt down before her. "There's no one outside, no one else coming to get him. You can put the knife down."

"No!" At her outburst, the baby began crying loudly. She picked him up and began rocking again. "Swear you won't tell anyone!"

He phrased his words carefully. "Nobody else will know. You'll be protected so that no person can take him from you."

"If anybody comes to get him, I'll kill him first—" Shuta paused— "even if he is my nephew, I'll kill him before anybody else can have him. Your mother comes, I'll kill her, too."

"*Ohan.* Yes, I believe you." He could see tragedy unfolding before his eyes. Iná, who been almost comical on a rampage in the hospital nursery—he could see her in a death struggle with Shuta, unwilling to give up her grandson at any cost—two furious Lakota women so locked in a fight that they'd forget the baby—his son. Or three: Iná and Tate working together at last, one to get Shuta, the other to get her son. It would seem so easy. So brave. It would be a slaughter. He must not let it happen.

He began singing the same Lakota lullaby she'd been singing when he arrived, singing it softly, over and over until she joined in.

"See? You must take care of him now. And to do that, you must take care of yourself as well. End the mourning, wash your face, heal your cuts." He reached out, so close to his son he could feel the wailing, as if his son knew he was being left. He reached out to touch the arm holding the knife.

She let him stroke salve into her gashes. She didn't quiver. Shuta, like her name, was tough. He must be tougher. He could wrest the knife from her easily now—but what would be the point? He'd given his Word: he'd given his son into the hands of the Great Mystery.

CHAPTER 28
TATE

Pine Ridge Hospital, Tate's Room, dawn

TATE LOOKED up from her sleep. Someone was in the room, rummaging around in her locker. A nurse's aide trying to steal her maternity clothes? No, the backside of a flowered dress, one of the grammas. Oh, no, Iná.

"Did you find my baby? I was knocked out and didn't see my baby at birth, and afterwards they didn't tell me." She burst into tears. "I haven't seen her. I asked, but they keep saying to wait—"

"Yes, we saw him," she said, "and I got the *tun*." Iná handed the black lizard beaded leather bag to her. "Hold onto it tight. Don't lose it in the hospital. It's a boy. But don't cry. Save your green turtle beaded bag for the next baby."

Tate felt the bulge in the bag. Could that have once been inside her, part of the birth cord? What was it called, *chekpa oganake?*

"Better yet," Iná said, "hide it inside unfinished cradleboard, where no one will look."

All those tiny black beads spread out, gleaming with life. A boy. Alex would be happy, too. She handed the bag to Iná, who tied it in the cradleboard out of sight.

Then Iná looked down at her, frowning. "You don't look good. Better come home and let us doctor you." She brushed Tate's hair back. Her touch wasn't fierce, but gentle.

Could Iná be feeling sorry for her? She wished for a moment that she'd listened to her, who wanted a midwife to deliver the baby at home. If that had happened, she'd have seen her baby emerge and would have been able to hold him. "But where's Alex?"

"Looking for the doctor, ready to take you out of here." Then Iná reached into her large satchel for bottles of—"I brought you some skeleton-plant tea to make your milk flow. Hide it somewhere out of the way so these White nurses won't throw it out. Drink it, it'll make your womb shrink, go back in place. Chew roots of slender milk vetch. Better than those drugs they give you that wipe you out, like I saw you just now, drugged into restless sleep, not getting better."

Tate looked down into Iná's satchel. More bottles. More herbs. Deerskin.

"When we bring you home, this is what you must do:
Bathe baby with tepid water boiled in dry sage leaves.
Wipe baby dry with soft deerskin.
Rub with buffalo fat or red ochre to keep baby skin moist.
Red paint to show baby from the *pte oyate*, the Buffalo Calf People.
Wrap baby in soft deerskin.
Never leave baby uncovered."

No diapers. No talcum powder. No bottles of milk. No pacifiers.

Ina continued, "Rest four days, keep baby near, nursing him while you rest. *Azikhiya ye*, so you let baby suck at breast right away. If no milk, I bring you milk vetch to chew or drink tea from skeleton plant."

Oh no. Tate said, "No more teas."

"Put baby on stomach so the new sacred being can stare wide-eyed at you, dark eyes alert and curious to see Lakota world filled with order and beauty. In White World, they call it Mother-bonding."

"Now you *hokshikigna*," Iná announced. "Now you soothe baby to sleep, hum or chant songs. I teach you one called 'Be still, sleep.' Follow after me: *A wa wa wa, inila ishtima na.*"

Fortunately Tate knew at least one word: *ishtima*. Sleep was all she could think about. All around her someone was singing.

In her dream Tate heard the door to her room bang open. She woke up. "Alex?"

Iná rushed to close the door. Instead, one of the hospital doctors at last to tell her about her baby. Iná tried to block him from her view, but Tate recognized him as the same white-haired man that Buster had recognized when Iná's house had been wrecked.

He said, "I've come to inspect—"

Iná interrupted. "Out!" She pushed him back towards the open door. "Wrong room. This is Maternity."

He grabbed for Iná, who stepped back to protect Tate. "You in the pink nurses' aide uniform! You're the one I caught you searching for drugs, and I'll turn you in."

Out came Iná's diamond willow cane, *whack-whack*, advancing on the man. "You in the fake doctor's coat and badge, retired with cowboy boots and fake rodeo belt." *Whack-whack.* "I know you from way back twenty years ago at your clinic in Philip."

Dr. White Hair, backing toward the door, looked at Tate. "Don't you have your baby to feed? He picked up a bottle that earlier she had thrown on the floor. "It's unsterile now," he said. And left, closing the door on Iná.

She whispered to Tate, "He was thin and young, had a head full of hair when he delivered *Misun*. You saw him bend down and look under the bed?" asked Iná. "He after the *tun*?"

Her Ghost Man had told her that at the accident an 'inspector' had climbed down to look at the wreck. "No, I think he wanted Dr. Belva's black briefcase full of affidavits for the lawsuit." Tate hesitated. "Can that old doctor really turn you in?"

"No, we turn him in!" Whack-whack. "He head to elevator, press Down. Gonna steal records how he destroy us Indian women! I go downstairs and catch him." Whack-whack.

CHAPTER 29

ALEX

Camp Crazy Horse Ceremony House, near dawn

AFTER LEAVING Shuta, Alex had driven back to Camp Crazy Horse and parked the Midwife Express behind the Ceremony House. He entered to pray at the altar in the Ceremony House for his son's safety. And then fell asleep.

~~~

He woke to the sound of a pickup. Inside was dark, the windows covered with blankets from the previous ceremony. When he pulled back a blanket he saw Sonny's dark green pickup parked behind the Ceremony House. Hadn't the AIM guys stopped him at the Sundance grounds? Sonny knew better than to come back to Camp Crazy Horse, let alone the Ceremony House while drunk.

A figure slumped in the driver's side. He yanked the pickup door open to stop Sonny from climbing out of the cab. Instead it was the last person he'd expect: Shuta. Who'd stolen his baby son and threatened to kill him rather than give him back. Had she brought him after all?

"The Great Mystery must have changed your mind, Shuta. You brought Baby Joe back." Then he noticed her empty lap and bruised arms, tear-streaked face and reddened eyes. Shuta, who never cried. It was too much to expect, that she would have changed her mind and returned his son. So what was she doing here?

Before he could ask, Shuta climbed out of the pickup and thrust a medicine bundle of prayer ties and tobacco into his hands. "I'd bring you a pipe if I had one."

He thrust the offerings back at her. "Where's my son? How dare you not bring him?"

She turned her head, refusing to accept the tobacco ties, which fell to the ground. "Help me get Lester back."

"Your brother Lester is dead, Shuta."

"I mean Lester, Junior! My baby's gone!"

Shuta still believed Lester's lie that he had 'counted coup' on Tate. Alex knew he himself was the father of Tate's baby, conceived soon after their marriage. "Where's Baby Joe?"

Shuta grabbed Alex's arms as if to shake him into action. "After you left, *he* came, beat me up and took my baby away," she wailed. "You have to help me get him back."

He pushed her arms away. "Who?"

"Zack, the guy in the Morgue that looks like you."

"Why would he take a baby?"

"Because it's yours. He wants to hurt you."

When he'd seen this Zack in the hospital Morgue, he'd felt no ill will from him. Was Shuta making up another story to hide her neglect? "Where'd he go?"

"I don't know where Zack took him. He wants a trade."

"Ransom?" Alex felt his son slipping further away from him, from a jealous Shuta to Zack. He glared at her. "Does he live in the hospital housing?"

Shuta glared back. "He tricked me. He got me to take Lester Jr. from the nursery just so he could steal him from me."

Alex felt no sympathy for Shuta. Her cousin Patty worked in the hospital nursery, so stealing his son would have been easy. He headed to Iná's Midwife Express. He'd search all of Pine Ridge until he found his son.

Shuta rushed after him. "I have your knife."

Once Lakota women bit a knife to show they were speaking the truth. He knew that wasn't what Shuta had in mind.

Nor what he had in mind: confront this Zack himself. Alone.

He walked back to Sonny's pickup. In the early dawn light he saw the red prayer ties and tobacco pouch that she'd thrown on the ground. She'd been that desperate, that angry.

Shuta followed him. "Help me get my baby back, and you can have your damned knife."

To confront this Zack, he'd need his grandpa's hawk knife. So he took the knife from her hand and slipped it into his belt. "You can help if you admit that Baby Joe is Tate's and my son."

Shuta looked down, silent, stubborn. "Zack has a knife, too. A switchblade. You need me along. I know where he lives."

He'd find this Zack himself. She was too fierce. She'd start a knife fight, maybe slash both of them and take his son away again.

He pointed at her offerings. "Too bad these are wet."

Shuta, humbled, knelt and gathered red prayer ties in her hands. She handed them to him.

"I'll take these to the trash pile," he said. "It's almost dawn. Why don't you come inside and make new ones?"

Shuta hesitated, then sat down on the women's side bench.

He handed her his tin box for making prayer ties. "Use anything you need to make ten new offerings. Put them on the Ceremony House altar and pray for the baby you've lost."

While Shuta bent her head to place pinches of tobacco on small red cotton squares and tie them into knots on a string, he quietly removed the distributer cap from Smokey's green pickup.

Next he revved the engine of the Midwife Express and left for Pine Ridge Morgue in a spray of mud.

CHAPTER 30
TATE

Pine Ridge Hospital, Tate's room, morning

TATE WAS frantic. "Oh, Ghostman, where is Dr. Belva? I need her. I looked in the other rooms and she's not there. Iná is gone. Alex is gone. My baby's gone. How can Dr. Belva be gone, too? Oh, Ghost Man, I need her as a lawyer to get my baby back."

He said nothing, simply put a cool string of metal around her neck. She looked down to see silver squash blossoms. Dr. Belva's necklace. Which she always wore.

She remembered the wreck. Dr. Belva on the downside, crushed between the steering wheel and car's broken windows.

He leaned over and straightened the necklace. "In her last moments, these were her protection. She was protecting you."

Tate cried. "Ghost Man, who are you really?"

"My name is Ben. Belva's twin brother."

"I noticed that you were shadowing us. Even at the wreck."

I was following you, but you took a different route, so I shadowed him to see what he was up to. He sped up a paved road and then barreled down that same gravel road to drive my sister off and kill her."

180

Tate reached out to touch his hand, to comfort his sorrow. It brought back memories of Dr. Belva teasing her about passing 100% on the GED. Stuffing affidavits into the black briefcase at WARN. Crawling into the old bunkers at Wounded Knee. Surviving Iná's stare over owl feathers. Tate said, "You went back to get the black briefcase so the lawsuit can continue."

Ben was silent. At last he said, "I got to bless her body, wrap her in sheets and carry her to the ambulance. Now it's as if I have only one lung to breathe, only one eye to see."

CHAPTER 31

ALEX

Pine Ridge Hospital Morgue, morning

ALEX PARKED the Midwife Express at the rear of the dark and almost empty hospital parking lot. Tate was lying upstairs in the maternity ward, but he couldn't face her yet, not until he'd found his son. Still, going down into the Morgue, the House of the Dead, couldn't be any worse. He yanked open a side door, ran down the steps to the basement and entered the dark corridor, archives at one end, where he'd been yesterday with Iná, and at the other end, the Morgue. Zack had to be inside.

He paused before the door to calm himself. He'd been full of rage, rage at Shuta, rage at his own helplessness, and underneath, fear. Fear of the dark energy of the dead. Fear he'd never see his son again, just that one glimpse of him lying asleep in a bassinette in the nursery above. He'd been so brave earlier, trusting in *Wakan Tanka* the Great Mystery to protect his son. Now he prayed that *Wakan Tanka* would protect him from his own killing rage.

He clutched sage underneath his shirt, next to his heart, opened the steel door and looked around. Inside was cool, as before when he'd brought Hokshicala in, and still smelled of alcohol and cigarettes and metal. Hair at the back of his neck rose. In the big room he sensed a sharp disquieting energy, not repose, even though it was empty.

He knew that the Morgue attendant had used Shuta to steal the baby for him. But what did the man want?

A light glowed in the back hallway. "Anybody here?" he called, and strode past the metal tables, some covered with draped cloth, toward the back. A dark figure emerged, shadowed by the light from behind, wearing a gray plastic apron over green hospital garb.

As the man strode forwards, Alex saw what Shuta had meant. The man looked like himself, except for his tattooed hands and scarred face.

"Can I help you?" The voice sounded flat and polite, but the lips sneered. A metal stretcher lay between them.

Alex held his body in check. "Your name is Zack."

"Yes. Zack comes back."

"Shuta says you have my son. I want him."

"Fuck, you believe that ranting *puta*?" Zack shook his head. "She said it's her brother's baby, called him Lester Junior. But he's a Turning Hawk. Turning Hawk nose, like you and me."

Lies. Zack must be part of part of a Mafia baby selling ring. Drugs and babies. Black market. Alex reached across and pushed him in the chest. "You stole my son."

"Hey, chulo, I did you a favor. Moccasin Telegraph has it you already found your son once, and you let that fucking crazy puta keep him! A little thing like a knife at the throat scared you off." Zack pushed Alex back. "That wouldn't have stopped me! And I'm only his uncle."

"Uncle?" More lies. Alex had no brothers. Iná had only one child. He shoved the stretcher into Zack's gut.

"Yes, dear fucking Alex." The name echoed off the metal walls. "I'm Zack, Zachariah, like in the Bible, your long-lost brother, come home at last." He shoved the stretcher back. "Ask your mother who I am. She knows."

Could his father have had another son? But he'd been gone for years; some even said he drank himself to death. Alex stepped around the stretcher, came closer. "How much money?"

Zack stepped right up to his face. "I want my Turning Hawk name and my share of Turning Hawk land."

Alex felt a chill. Zack had been out on their land. At the vision pit, leaving a dead baby in a black cradleboard. At the big cabin, leaving black tobacco ties on the red hard by the door. At the ceremony house, black tobacco ties on the altar. At Iná's house in town, leaving owl feathers in between Tate's piano strings. Zack had been everywhere, yet no one had seen him. So invisible he could be a *wanaghi,* a ghost spirit returned from the dead, bringing death. No wonder he could work with the dead. Alex shook himself clear of the images and backed off. "You want a trade. Baby for land. I—" Alex hesitated. Anything for his son. Yet the land was not his to trade.

"Half is mine. Get that bruja to recognize me and sign it over. When she comes to the Pine Ridge Land Office and signs the papers, you get your son back." Zack turned away and headed toward the lighted corridor.

"You won't get away with this blackmail!" Alex shouted at his back.

"Talk to your fucking mother. She knows it all, even if she never told you."

It was too much. Iná with her secrets. Alex vaulted over the metal stretcher between them, grabbed the ponytail and flung Zack to the floor, banging his head. Before Zack could turn over, Alex whipped out a calf-tying rope and tied Zack's hands behind his back. Zack lashed out with steel-tipped boots. But Alex, used to ornery calves and wilder broncos, managed to bind Zack's ankles together.

"Where is he? Where do you have him hidden?" To stop the loud nonstop swearing, Alex pulled a sheet off a nearby stretcher, stuffed a corner into Zack's mouth, wrapped the rest around him and dragged him back into the corridor. He kicked open a broom closet door and pushed Zack inside.

Then he vented his rage. He yanked open cooler drawers, only to find dead bodies inside. Banging the draped stretchers together, he raced past the muffled cursing coming from the broom closet, past a bathroom, to a door at the very rear of the corridor. Catching his breath, he felt his son close by. Inside. The door was locked.

Before he could kick it in, Alex heard the broom closet door bang open. He turned to face an enraged Zack, loose with a switchblade in his right hand.

In his haste Alex had missed the knife hidden in the biker boots. He backed against the corridor wall, balancing on his toes, hands at the ready. Just like the time a charging bull had cornered him against the rodeo stands—either duck and avoid the hooves, or grab the horns and flip over his head and away.

Zack swaggered closer. "You're a rope man, I'm a knife man. Knife cuts rope. Now, medicine man, what're you gonna do? Hex me?" He flipped the switchblade closed, then click—open again.

Alex watched the hands as Zack danced back and forth, taunting him to come closer, just as that bull had tossed his sharp horns and pawed the earth with his sharp hooves.

"You're just a half-brother, so I won't kill you. I could mark you so you'd remember who I am. But I don't need to. It's me who has what you want. Did you forget?" Zack moved closer, an underhand jab ready.

Alex held out his right hand. "Do anything, just give my baby back to me."

"You want to shake my hand? You believe in honor? Okay, I'll give you my right hand, but I keep my blade in my left." Zack flipped the knife in the air and caught it. Then he offered his right hand to Alex. "Truce."

Alex shook it, a hand as big and worn as his own. "We each have our talents. If you are my brother, I will not harm you. Just as I trust you will not harm my son." He pointed to the locked door. "But he needs his mother to nurse him."

"He's safe, but he's not in there." Zack half-smiled. "You think I'm stupid? That's a storage room where I crash. Just a bed and a backpack." He shrugged his shoulders and said in a low voice, "I got no home, no land, only my Harley."

Zack was a sweet-talker, smooth and playing for sympathy. Feed a vicious bull a bale of hay, he's peaceful, for a while. Alex replied, "I can do nothing. The land is in Iná's name."

"You bring her to the hospital Chapel, sanctuary. I'll talk to her, remind her she's una abuela. She'll trade land to get her grandson back."

Alex doubted it. "You don't know how stubborn she is."

"But I do." Zack shoved Alex away from the door. "She's a mean son-of-a-bitch. After my mother died, your mother wouldn't take me in. I was four years old, and she put me on a bus alone, all the way from Rapid City to L.A. Sent me back to the Social Services."

CHAPTER 32
TATE

Pine Ridge Hospital, Tate's Room, late morning

TATE PROPPED Iná's traveling satchel, an old painted hide par-fleche, to keep the door open for Alex. She was sweaty, her eyes red, her cheeks wet. Wearing herself out with worry.

Finally Alex appeared, empty-handed. She pushed him away. "Where have you been all this time? We were ready to call the cops on you." She burst into tears. "Where's my baby? I've never even seen him!"

She should have been angry, but instead she wrapped him in her arms. "Look at you! Instead you've been in a fight. But you didn't find him?"

Alex pulled her close. "I found who took him—" then paused and asked, "Iná left you alone? When you might have done something stupid, like ripping open your stitches in your own frantic search for baby Joe?"

"She's gone after that fat old white doctor looking for the Records Room. He came in here looking for something under the bed, but she whacked him with her cane."

"The same Dr. White Hair that caught us in the Delivery Room?"

"Iná called him by a different name, Dr. Erikson, because she recognized him from before. She chased him into the elevator. She's on the warpath to kill him for what he did to her."

Alex looked puzzled. "How could I have missed her? I just came from the Morgue.

Tate shrieked. "My baby's at the Morgue?"

"Our baby! No, he's not. I've fought the truth out of my half-brother Zack. He looks like me. He has Baby Joe. Now that he's of age, he's come to get his share of the land. He wants my mother to sign over the papers to the Turning Hawk allotment. In exchange for our son."

"He must be lying. Why didn't you make him take you to where Baby Joe's hidden?"

Alex pulled the extra chair close to the bed, opposite her. He reached out and took both of her hands so they formed a family ring. He felt the slow, drugged pulse of Tate, the tremor in his own. "We need to work this out together."

She stifled a sigh. "Iná told me you were her only child."

"Até, my father, who I can't remember. Who disappeared from our lives when I was two. She said she kicked him out for drinking."

Tate nodded.

"But what really happened is that Até found another woman." Alex continued. "Iná knew when she saw the burned cradleboard with the pink and green beadwork. That's why she insisted on burying the dead baby with the cradleboard as well."

Tate asked, "So when the mother died, this Zack was adopted out, instead?".

"Social Services tried. They sent him to Iná when he was four, but she put him on a bus back to L.A."

So Iná had been *tawachin shicha*. Stingy-hearted. Done something so shameful, turned away a blood relation—especially an orphan only four years old. "Once, she told me that she'd never raise a whore's son, but I didn't understand what she meant."

"If people learn of this, Tate, my proud mother will be forced to walk out the door, walk away from us, even from a grandson—forever."

"She's going to kill that doctor, which is even worse." Tate laughed bitterly. "The Great Mystery works in unknowable ways," she said, remembering his usual phrase. "So Shuta stole Baby Turning Hawk for your half-brother, only to have him steal my baby back to use as a pawn to claim Turning Hawk land."

CHAPTER 33
ALEX

Pine Ridge Hospital Morgue, noon

WHERE COULD Iná have gone? He took the elevator down to the Morgue. It was closed and locked. No Zack. But Ben Thundercloud was there instead. "Why are you here?" Alex asked.

Ben thumped on the glass door. "My sister's in there. I need to see how she was treated."

Alex remembered that Belva had died in the wreck, and how Ben had wept in his pickup.

"Have you seen my mother? The woman with the cane?"

"I missed her. A white-haired doctor came down—Dr. White Hair, the one Iná was chasing, and ran into the Morgue attendant," Ben added. "The doctor offered him greenbacks for the key ring to the Records Room. The guy took the money and vanished. I need those keys."

How could Zack have vanished? Was there another way out besides the elevator and the stairs down to the Morgue? "But where's my mother? She's after hospital records from the fifties for your sister's lawsuit."

Pine Ridge Hospital Records Room, noon

Alex and Ben ran to the end of the corridor and turned the corner. Too late. The Records Room door had been flung open. Files were scattered all over the floor. Had there been a fight? Had Iná accosted Dr. White Hair? "Hear anything while you were down here?"Alex asked. "I'm afraid for my mother, who might flail her cane at a man she once knew." Who might be even more desperate than Iná.

"There must be another way out of here," Ben said. He ran to the far end of the corridor and yanked open a door. Dead end. A closet."

"Hey," called Alex. "Behind this desk there's a broken casement window." Alex brushed glass shards away from the desk, which had been pushed up to the window. Documents had been laid to cover the broken slices. Outside was only scraped earth.

Dr. White Hair must have found his old medical records and stolen them, revealing his part in the sterilization of Lakota women. How had that fat retired man squeezed himself out? They could follow easily.

"That man killed my sister," Ben cried, wriggling through first.

Alex quickly followed. They brushed dirt off and stared. In the distance, Iná, beside her Midwife Express, held a red two-gallon can of gas in one hand, and with the other, shook her cane at Dr. White Hair, who had climbed into his fancy tan rig and revved the motor.

Badlands National Monument, 1pm.

Alex ran after Ben to the far side of the hospital parking lot. They jumped into Ben's old pickup, but by the time they left the lot, the two vehicles ahead were dust on the trail, heading north into the Badlands.

After half an hour, nearing the chase—fence wire broken through—they followed the tire tracks onto a mesa. Iná stood beside the fancy pickup, raised a rifle and shot wildly at Dr. White Hair, headed downhill toward the Cheyenne River.

191

As they pulled up beside her, she lowered the rifle. "No need to shoot out tires on a gas-guzzler. You think I don't know how to sipe gas?" She shot another volley that echoed across the mesa. "Can't load a rifle and aim? All these years I feed you deer meat?" She paused. "I take his rifles away while he in Records Room. He not remember me, but I scare him."

Ben jumped out of his pickup and started running after the doctor.

Iná handed the empty rifle to Alex. "I shoot around that doctor, make him dance until I run out." She reached into the Midwife Express and pulled out a second rifle."This one still loaded," she said as she peppered the dirt around Ben. "Navajo medicine man, you want to dance, too?"

Ben walked back up to them. "He killed my sister."

Iná replied, "Car wreck an accident."

Ben grabbed the second rifle from her. "No accident. It was deliberate. I was there behind him and saw it all, unable to stop it—until now. I get to choose his fate."

Alex said, "Drop the rifle, Ben. We need him alive to testify at the lawsuit hearing. Make him confess and be sorry." His canny mother had left Ben an empty rifle for the Navajo medicine man to decide. Let them have at it.

Iná picked up the first rifle and aimed at him. "Stop!" she cried. "You want to throw him off a cliff? This is MY victory. What about my fate? My only son stands before you. No more kids, I should cut his balls off—but no, he too old to have any. I got my revenge: papers for the lawsuit, briefcase full of affidavits, plus files of doctors' records for evidence of genocide." She lowered her rifle and pointed at the rifle Ben held.

"You want eye for eye—that empty rifle kill many men - see the notches? Let him drown in the river, or if he make it across, he step into Gunnery Range full of unexploded ammo. He a pitiful old man."

Ben replied, "Not so pitiful. I count seven notches."

"Mr. Ben, I took your sister in," Iná said. "She high class. Taught my daughter, an orphan, who I make as my own daughter. You cure her with honey. So we finish what your sister started, take briefcase affidavits, medical records for the lawsuit. Safe now in my Midwife Express."

Ben stared at the notched rifle in his hands. He turned away, sat down, and howled.

Like Smokey in the sweat lodge had howled with his son. Alex bent down to touch Ben.

Iná shook her head. "When women cry, we circle around to comfort them. Men, best to leave them alone. I got back the black briefcase and hospital records from 1950-60. We finished." She grabbed Alex by the arm. *"Misun,* carry them to my car. We got other things to settle, no more time. I got one more person to scare."

CHAPTER 34

ALEX

Pine Ridge Hospital Chapel - morning

ALEX STOOD with Tate and Iná at the entrance to the hospital Chapel. Its two stained glass windows remained dark. Only one candle on the altar lit the room. Zack wasn't there. The emptiness of the Chapel echoed the terrible premonition in Alex's heart that Zack wouldn't bring baby Joe, or worse, wouldn't show up at all. He'd been so hopeful when he'd convinced his wife and mother to meet Zack. For their sakes he had to keep positive. "Zack said he'd be here. Let's sit down in front of the altar. If we hang around the door, he might not come."

Tate took his hand, walking in rustling paper slippers, ready to follow him. They walked down to the altar, where he laid his string of red tobacco tie offerings next to the votive candle. Each tie was a prayer to God, in Alex's own way asking for help to recover baby Joe. The candle had a Catholic saint on its side, but it didn't matter to him. Prayers were prayers, whatever language or tradition; only pure intent counted.

But Iná did not join them. She clutched her satchel in both hands and blocked the entrance. "I wait at the door to catch him first, before he enters this Christian place."

Stubborn old woman. He knew his mother felt the chapel was an alien place. There was no use dragging her down to the altar to pray.

"Focus on the light," Tate said in a steady voice, "until we become of one mind. Forget everything else but baby Joe. Pray together for his safe return." The fragrant smell of sage and kinnick-kinnick, red willow tobacco, filled the room. Each tie was a prayer to God, in his own way asking for help to recover baby Joe.

"Guess he ain't coming," Iná called down to him, still blocking the entrance.

Just then Alex caught a glimpse of movement in the dark Chapel. A closet door in the left wall opened slightly, and in the gloom a person's shape appeared. He'd come.

Tate picked up the votive candle and walked toward him. "Welcome, Zack."

Alex's heart plummeted. Zack had come empty-handed.

Iná raced down the aisle and rushed up to Zack. "Not a Christian. Here, it don't bother me. No more talk-talk. Three against one, no problem."

Ignoring both Alex and Tate with the candle, Zack faced Iná. "Now that I'm of age, I've come to get my half of the land. Sign the papers to the Turning Hawk allotment in exchange for your grandson."

Before Alex could stop her, Iná took an antique pistol from her satchel and pointed it at Zack's chest. The gun was bigger than Iná's hand. Probably captured in some Nineteenth Century battle. Probably no bullets, either. Good thing she'd left the rifles with Ben.

Iná waved her gun at Zack. "Take us to him!"

"Stop!" Alex wrested the pistol from his mother. "Which is more important, dear mother, the land or the baby? For my son, I give up my share."

Tate with her candle illuminated Iná's face like a skull.

Zack leaned toward Iná. "I ain't a Christian, neither," he said and laughed. "I seen lots of guns. That one ain't loaded." He reached behind his back and pulled out a derringer. "But this one is. Put yours away, you old buzzard."

"Go ahead, shoot me!" Iná shouted back. "That way you never get the land, you go straight to prison and it stays Turning Hawk land."

Alex stepped in between the two. Iná's pistol was so old and rusty it wouldn't fire even if loaded. Turning his back to her, he grabbed Zack's elbow and laid red prayer ties over Zack's derringer. "These are for you, *misun*."

The word *misun*, younger brother, echoed throughout the small Chapel.

Iná broke the silence first. "We protect the land. We never sell. We die first. The hang-around-the-forts who sold their land, what happens to them? They die later, crawling to White Clay in Nebraska for booze."

Zack dangled the red prayer ties in his left hand, kept the gun in his right, and said to Iná,

"You turned me away, yer own relation. Indian way, ain't that a crime?"

Alex cringed, thinking, don't embarrass her, or she'll walk out and we'll never get anywhere. He took the gun from his brother's left hand. "You're used to forcing your way to get what you want, so you took Baby Joe. But you didn't have to. We'll give you what you want."

Before Zack could say anything, Iná cried, "No! You brought death to our land, our home. You touch death every day."

Tate pushed past Iná and thrust the votive candle at him. "Zack, all I want is my baby."

Zack slipped the red prayer ties into his waistband and backed away. "I don't want your candle and I don't want your son."

Then he turned to Iná. "Old woman, my father's wife, I want you to recognize me, give me the Turning Hawk name, not the one Social Services gave me, and my share of the land."

Iná shook her head, holding her pistol at him.

Alex switched to Lakota to intervene. "*Misun* looks like me. I claim him as my brother, even though you told me I was your only child."

"Até," she replied. Father. She sidled backwards away from Alex and Zack.

"So Até found another woman?"

"*Ohan.*" Yes.

"Até, my father, who I can't remember. Who disappeared from our lives when I was two. You said you kicked him out for drinking."

She didn't answer.

"You knew there was another son?"

"*Hiya.*" No.

"But you knew when you saw the burned cradleboard with the pink and green beadwork from Black Eyes Camp." Alex continued relentlessly. "That's why you insisted on burying the dead baby with the cradleboard as well."

Her eyes drilled into him. "Got rid of it."

"But not him. Zack said his mother came and asked you to take him, but you refused."

"I'd never raise a whore's son."

"So when she died, he was adopted out, instead?"

"I never saw him." Iná smoothed her skirt again.

"But you knew his name. Zachariah, from the Bible."

She shrugged. "I never pay attention to that book."

"He says Social Services sent him to you at four, but you put him on a bus back to L.A."

"Who do you believe: him or your mother who birthed you and raised you?" Iná turned away to escape his words.

Stone-faced, Iná switched to English: "I raise my only son. To be honorable. Hard without a father. Now he turns against me."

Alex realized what his mother's words were hiding: *tawachin shicha.* Stingy-hearted. Once she had done something so shameful, turned away a blood relation—especially an orphan. If pressed, she would be forced to walk out the door, walk away from them forever.

Zack still had his gun. With all the wrangling, he realized that Tate had left the Chapel.

CHAPTER 35
TATE

Pine Ridge Hospital Nursery, morning

ZACK STILL had Baby Joe. The Chapel had a cold empty air, sepulchral. She'd felt so alone, left in the hospital, tied to a dripping needle. And now, when her baby was gone, arguing over land was useless. That half-brother Zack! She could have killed him. All that time he was stealing her baby to use as a pawn. Even though she'd never gotten the chance to see her baby, she knew with a mother's instinct that Zack hadn't brought Baby Joe along. Her son wasn't hidden in the Chapel's back room.

She inched away from the three still arguing, walked up the aisle in her rustling paper slippers to the door and left the chapel unnoticed, still holding her votive candle. If she prayed hard enough, the Great Mystery would help her, even if she was still bleeding and couldn't touch the Sacred Pipe or make tobacco ties.

She tuned out the talk-talk, more accusations and fighting. Her breasts began to drip milk, seeping through her hospital gown. She needed her son now. "Show me the way, lead me," she whispered. Walking down the corridor, her votive candle lighting the hospital corridors, she sensed that Baby Joe was somewhere inside, nearby. Not hidden in a linen closet, not hidden in an underground room in the Morgue, where crying would be noticed. No. Hidden in plain sight where crying would *not* be noticed: the hospital nursery. Probably under a different name wearing a different beaded bracelet.

She took the elevator to the second floor, turned into the Maternity Ward and walked the deserted hall to the Nursery. The day nurse's aide wasn't inside, probably taking a smoke break. A dozen babies slept in their bassinettes. She opened the door and entered the warm, dimly-lit room. She breathed in the sweetness of talcum powder, baby oil and flannel, matching her rhythm to the rising and falling sighs of newborns. Inhale. Exhale. Which one was Baby Joe?

She walked up and down the rows, still holding the candle, her eyes half-closed so she could feel rather than try to see her baby. Her aching breasts would lead her, dripping milk as she drew closer to where he lay hidden in plain sight. No, no, and no. Then, halfway down the third row, there he was, wrapped in pink, tiny thumb in tiny mouth, eyes closed in sleep, and a bump for a nose, the Turning Hawk nose in miniature. She read his baby bracelet: Lora Broken Rope?

Zack thought he was so clever. Without waking her son, she reached down and lifted him up underneath her gown. She slipped his thumb out and held his mouth to her breast until, without opening his eyes, he started sucking her nipple. Her whole body trembled at his touch, his hunger, his sweet warmth. She blew out the candle and laid it down in the empty bassinette. Holding her baby tightly to her body, she left the room and walked into the elevator and back down to the Chapel.

She stood at the open door, rocking back and forth so her baby would feel her body's rhythm, and switched breasts for him to nurse. Alex, Zack and Iná were at the altar, still fighting so loudly that they didn't notice her.

She heard Zack say, "Now that I'm of age, I've come back to get my half of the land. Sign over the papers to the Turning Hawk allotment. In exchange for your grandson."

And Alex's reply, "Which is more important, the land or the baby?"

She already had the answer in her hands. If only they would look up. Then Baby Joe opened his mouth and cried lustily. She walked down the aisle, past Iná and Zack, and handed her squalling son into Alex's arms.

CHAPTER 36
ALEX

Pine Ridge Hospital Chapel, morning

ALEX HELD his lost son Baby Joe tightly in his arms and rocked him back and forth until his son hushed and stared up at him. Eyes, liquid black and deep. He gazed into them, seeing the Great Mystery's miracle of birth for the first time.

Iná's mouth opened, but he couldn't hear. A tiny hawk nested in his arms. Hawk Power from the Great Mystery, "Kree–kree, kree–kree," echoed throughout the Chapel. Couldn't they hear it? Cradling his son, he rose into the air, past the stained glass windows, flew high into the bowl of sky so he could see with hawk-eye vision the whole Turning Hawk world below:

In the Badlands, Ben and the old doctor,

Old Sam in his hut,

Shuta holding another stolen baby,

Clarence asleep in Iná's shed—

Camp Crazy Horse, the warriors at the Sundance ground, smoking and laughing by the fire pit, rocks glowing red—

~~~

He unfolded his wings to let his son see it all, how the Camp would grow. Power from the Great Mystery filled his chest: to fly above, to see all below, to know what to do, to make the world right again, to bring back honor and generosity, courage and sharing. He, with Tate, had created life, a new being. He wrapped his wings around Baby Hawk, whose black eyes shone with the gift of *Wakan Tanka,* and flew back into the Chapel below.

Still cradling his son, Alex raised his voice. "These are the Turning Hawk and Camp Crazy Horse conditions:

"One. No guns. Dear Mother, you must hand over any other weapon to me."

Iná huffed. "I keep my Lakota woman butchering knife."

"Zack, Dear Brother, hand over your LA gang switchblade to Tate." Zack spread out his hands and bowed. "You're stripping me," he said, but handed it over.

Zack spread out his hands and bowed. "You're stripping me," he said, but handed it over.

"Two, no alcohol."

"Yes, Big Brother."

"Three, no dope."

"Yes, Big Brother."

Alex waited for Zack to finish bowing. He wanted to say, "Four, no whores," but he stopped. Four was the sacred number. He added the words on the car hood at the Camp Crazy Horse gate: "No cameras or tape recorders," and continued with a sacred prayer to the Great Mystery—"for the Land, for the People, for the Language, and for the Sundance to continue the next seven generations."

Finally he handed his son to Iná.

Iná's eyes sparkled. "*Mitakoja.* My grandson."

In return he wrested the diamond cane from his mother and pounded it on the stone floor for silence. "Iná, for my son, I'll give up my share. Tate and I have already agreed to this. Now we keep our word: Turning Hawk Honor. He took his son from Iná and gave him to Tate.

"Hechetuelo." So it is.

Iná faced Zack, stared him down, and finally said, "You get one-fourth the land. The pines to the west. Still sacred land. And I get all my conditions. Okay?"

"Yes, Iná," his half-brother smiled and bowed slightly.

"You agree without knowing them?" Iná shook her head.

Zack kept repeating, "Yes, Iná," over and over again. But Alex knew that those two would squabble in town, while at Camp Crazy Horse all would be well.

Alex didn't trust the wide smile Iná gave Zack. He knew his mother as a canny trader. Nor did he trust Zack's obsequious bowing. Let the two outfox each other.

Then he realized that, of course, Iná wasn't finished. He thumped the diamond willow cane on the stone floor again.

She stood beside him. "Be careful of that cane, made by your father." Then she grabbed Zack's hands and pursed her lips toward Tate, Baby Joe and himself. "They get my grandson. I get you."

"Yes, Iná," His half-brother bowed and swung her around.

"I'm getting old, kinda lonely, need lotsa help. You're kinda skinny-looking, I fatten you up on *papa,* drymeat and frybread. Learn you Lakota."

"Yes, Iná." Zack smiled broadly.

"I ain't finished. My last condition: you keep calling me 'old woman.' Now you get to call me 'Iná.' In Lakota, that means 'Mother.'"

Zack smiled again. "No problem, Iná."

Zack should have called his new mother '*Unchishi*,' the respectful Lakota term for 'mother-in-law,' but he'd begin to learn what he'd gotten into. He heard Tate laugh, too, because she'd already learned what that word meant.

CHAPTER 37
TATE

Pine Ridge Hospital Chapel, late morning

TATE SHOOK Zack with a mother's fury. "Now it's my turn. Why'd you steal my baby?"

"What's most dear? Zack replied, "How else could I claim my father's inheritance, name, and land?"

Lots of ways, she thought. What other pitiful tale would he spin now.

"You already know Iná rejected me, put me back on the bus to LA. As well as that my father left and then my mother burned up in a house fire. I crawled out with only my cradleboard and was sent to nearest relative in South Dakota. Then Indian Services fostered me out—you know what that means—to an Italian family, grew up on the streets, running errands. Fights, gangs. My foster father ran one, so learned to promote all kinds of drugs. A small kid can run fast, duck through cops' legs, hauled in as a runaway, then back to my foster father, until he, too, kicked me out. I lived then on the streets. Survived."

"So the dead baby, the one Alex calls Hokshicala, is yours?"

"Never heard that name."

"You grew up as part of a gang, got the Boss's daughter pregnant, got thrown out, left the pregnant girl and took off by motorcycle to Pine Ridge—" Tate stopped and asked, "Why'd he kick you out, when you were his slickest runner?"

"I grew up beside his daughter. She loved me."

"You got her pregnant."

"I loved her. Wanted to marry her."

"But wasn't she only fifteen, and your foster father kicked you out?"

"I didn't know she was pregnant, and when I did, the Boss kicked me out, just me and my cradleboard. No mama, no clothes, no toys, all burned up."

"Wait a minute—that was when you were four, not fourteen. Or eighteen. You had to run from Him. The Boss. Ran to the Res to hide out. You stole a buddy's cycle. Stole his stash."

"To get even with your hag of a mother-in-law, claim my inheritance and my Turning Hawk name. Found a job no one else wanted, easy pay, easy hours, a cubbyhole to crash."

"So now your old girlfriend found you out and dropped the dead baby at the Morgue where you work?"

"Her baby. Dropped by one of the chulos. How could I know it was mine?"

"Your baby. Dead or alive?"

"Dead. It belonged at the Morgue."

"You used your dead baby to terrorize us with black tobacco ties, desecrate all the sacred Turning Hawk places. Just to get even with Iná?"

"Yeah, her."

Tate wondered who would get even with whom. She turned away and cradled her baby, ready to nurse again. "I will always remember that you stole my baby. So don't expect to play Uncle with him."

CHAPTER 38
TATE

Pine Ridge Courthouse, next day, morning

INÁ TOOK over. Because the Great Mystery had saved her grandson's life, Iná had changed her mind and signed an affidavit for the lawsuit. She rounded up Tate with Baby Joe in his cradleboard as her witness, and marched up the Pine Ridge Courthouse steps.

Iná laughed bitterly. "Now I get my revenge, twenty years later. Lawsuit. Affidavits. I will get other women in town to agree to testify in a Lakota way to cover shame. Not their fault. Not my fault. Not even Até's fault."

Marcus Big Tree, the tribal lawyer, signed and sealed her affidavit.

Next, Iná rousted Zack Espada, her new son, from his lair in the Morgue. With Tate as a witness, she took him by the arm to the Tribal Land Office to register him as Zack Turning Hawk, a tribal member and land owner of forty acres, up in the pines. Tate, along with Alex, had easily agreed to share their half of the land.

So long as he stayed up there, Tate thought, Zack, playing uncle, had gone ga-ga with Baby Joe and wanted to hold him. Un-uh. "You held him once—as ransom. Once is enough."

CHAPTER 39
ALEX

Pine Ridge Hospital Morgue, next day, morning

ALEX AND Ben removed Belva's body from the Morgue. Ben took a tanned sheep hide from his pickup. Together they wrapped her in it with sage and sweetgrass and laid her carefully in Ben's pickup. Then Alex blessed the bundle with the Turning Hawk Peace Pipe.

Before he left, Ben gave Alex his concho belt, honey and pollen.

Alex passed on his grandpa's hawk knife.

Iná appeared with a red two-gallon can of gas. "Can't stop on the way," she said.

Tate gave Ben their wedding star quilt to wrap Dr. Belva in for her return home. "This is a Wedding star quilt," she said to Ben, "my Ghost Man healer. So you must wear it to lead you to the person you will marry. Soon you'll have two lungs to breathe and two eyes to see."

CHAPTER 40
TATE

Camp Crazy Horse, three days later

AFTER THE piano was moved back into their log cabin, cream cans filled with fresh water from the stream, and commodity food stashed in the cupboards, Tate felt home at last. She and Alex were so relieved that they'd be left alone (maybe) with Baby Joe, who was now laced into his own almost-finished cradleboard with the beaded lizard bag dangling on top.

She could hardly believe that Iná had changed, to being tender toward her. Would Iná be a real mother to her at last? "I know the baby is mine," she'd told Iná. "Spirit People told me."

The Prodigal Son had returned, even if Iná didn't go by the Bible. She had adopted him as her second son, though he didn't realize that soon he would become her slave. She put on a *wopila* ceremony for Eagle Nest. Zack was honored at the welcoming feast at Turning Hawk's and given an Indian name. Tate wore her only jewelry, Dr. Belva's silver squash blossom necklace. She reluctantly handed Zack the cleaned and re-beaded Black Cradleboard, knowing it had been his only memory of Até. But she would never forget that he had stolen Baby Joe.

All was well—until Iná and Zack got into it.

Tate also discovered that Smokey had found a new cook for Camp Crazy Horse warriors, and a mother for Jerome Jr.—Flossie? Flossie sober? How long would that last? Had she brought Buster? Tate raced over to the campgrounds by the Sundance arbor to greet her old friend, and perhaps, now with two women at the camp, they could start a women's Sweat Lodge as well.

All the warriors took sweat together, to prepare for the Sacred Sundance that summer. Even Tim New Holy, the Tribal cop who brought Clarence to Camp Crazy Horse's gate, left his gun in his cruiser. He, too, headed for the Sweat Lodge.

Alex knew that in Navajo country another burial was taking place as well. He and Tate would never forget Belva. Tate had already registered for college, determined to become, like Belva, a People's lawyer. So when the sacred Sweat Lodge door was closed, the Camp Crazy Horse warriors, led by Alex, sent a Lakota prayer song all the way to Navajo land for Ben and his family.

~~~

When Clarence arrived at Camp Crazy Horse, he took over the Gate. "Better the living than the dead. Better food, too," he said. As a watchman, he began installing plyboards to protect the Camp's Security arbor from the sun and wind, ready for Sundance, where he took command. He told Alex, "If your father comes by, I will let him in."

CHAPTER 41
ALEX

Episcopal Church Cemetery, four days later

ALEX STOOD in full regalia amid the family. Hokshicala was now recognized as a Turning Hawk, and must be reburied where he belonged: inside the Turning Hawk cemetery plot, to sleep forever in the Spirit World. But not without a Turning Hawk name.

Iná and Tate had cleansed Hokshicala with soap weed, powdered with 'tree ears,' caressed with powdered marrow and bergamot, and had laid him to rest in a tiny carved wooden casket, now sitting on the grass beside them.

He lifted the Turning Hawk Pipe and called to his brother, Zack, "Stand beside me to give Hokshicala his real name."

"What do you mean?" Zack looked at the small empty grave.

Alex took his brother's hand. "The name I gave him, 'Hokshicala' means 'Little Baby Boy.' All this time I've called him that, because he was lost and buried without a name."

Zack let go of Alex's hand. "I never knew what his mother called him."

"He's your son. You must name him so he will rest in the Spirit World."

"We can call him Junior."

The graveyard was silent. Alex handed Zack the Turning Hawk Pipe. "Honor him now."

Zack held the ancient pipe and looked at the Turning Hawk graves. He looked at the small Turning Hawk clan around him, Iná and Tate. Then he said, "Okay, Alex. I give him our father's name, the name you've never heard: James."

HECHETUELO.
So Be It.

Historical References &
Contemporary Articles

THE MOST complete account is the following:

- "American Indian Culture & Research Journal," 24:2 (2000), p. 1-22.
- "Native American Women & Coerced Sterilization: On the Trail of Tears in the 1970s," Sally J Torpy.

Dr. Connie Uri, a Chocktaw-Cherokee physician working in California, uncovered a large-scale program for the sterilization of Native American women without their consent. She discovered that the records of the BIA-run Indian Health Service Hospital in Clairmont, OK, revealed that **75%** of their sterilizations were nontheraputic; some women thought it a reversible birth control; others groggily signed consent forms while sedated after childbirth. (Akwesasne Notes, 1974:22.)

Following Dr. Uri's lead, Senator James Abourezk initiated a federal investigation of the General Accounting Services hospitals.

According to the GAO report, between 1973 and 1976, over 3400 sterilizations were performed; 3000 on Indian women from the ages of 15 to 44. Not once were women offered consent forms. Four years later Senator Abourezk's Bill, "The Indian Child Welfare Act," passed in Congress.

Further studies revealed that the Indian Health Service sterilized between 25 and 50%. Cheyenne Tribal Judge Marie Sanchez found that *half* of Native women questioned had been sterilized. Mary Ann Bear Comes Out of the Northern Cheyenne, found that over three years, fifty-six of 165 questioned, nearly ⅔ had been sterilized.

Two lawsuits followed: In 1977 a Class Action Suit vs. HEW was brought by Michael Zavalla, a Tuscon attorney and three Northern Cheyenne women, including Bea Medicine, but there was no trial, only a cash settlement. In 1978 & 1980, Lee Brightman with the help of Marie Sanchez, filed suits against IHS, but again, none of the plaintiffs would go public.

- Eugenics: The Scalpel and the Sword: The Sterilization Campaign Targeting Native Americans in the 1970s.
- Charles R. England, A Look at the Indian Health Service Policy of Sterilization, 1972-1976.

Both tubal litigations and hysterectomies were used, despite such practices were rare among healthy young Native women.

- "First Nations Women forced to be sterilized before they could see newborns." Indian Country Today 11/27/2018
- Film about Forced Sterilizations of Indigenous Women by Mary Annette Pember.
- World-wide: Canada's Indigenous Women, Latinas in Los Angeles, Indigenous in Peru.

Sample chapter from the next Lakota Mystery

PEYOTE FIREBIRD

A Lakota Mystery

CHAPTER 1
ALEX TURNING HAWK

Camp Crazy Horse
Pine Ridge Reservation
April, 1978

CHASKÉ, THE youngest of his AIM warriors, wasn't missing. His pony was in the corral. His clothes were in his small tipi. But he wasn't around to haul logs and dig postholes to fence in Camp Crazy Horse for a buffalo herd. He wasn't around to sing and pray in the sweat lodge after a good day's work. On the Res a boy became a man by fourteen, so Alex Turning Hawk sent for his nephew.

It was April on the prairie. After a below-zero winter, the meadowlarks were back. Alex welcomed the sun warming the new grass. His wife Tate hung wool blankets on the clothesline to air. His son Baby Joe waved to him from his cradleboard strapped to her back. He hauled cream cans full of water into their log cabin for spring cleaning.

From a distance he heard the roar of an engine on the road, louder than a car. An older motorcycle - he could tell from its wheezing sputter - entered the camp and died in front of their log cabin. Chaské jumped off, propped the small Harley against the cabin wall. In a long loose whirl of black hair, his nephew avoided him standing in the doorway and strode over to Tate's back to tickle Baby Joe.

"Ka-ké," his son called, wiggling his arms to get loose. Baby Joe loved to play peek-a-boo with Chaské, who unlaced Baby Joe, held him in his arms and turned to face the cabin doorway. "Uncle, here I am."

Alex wasn't fooled by Chaské's swagger and clever use of his son as a security blanket. Chaské knew he'd been wrong to go AWOL. Instead of his army surplus parka and worn moccasins, Chaské wore a black leather jacket and biker boots. He'd changed into a faster world. But it wasn't too late to bring him back. Alex opened his arms. "Come in, nephew. We've missed you."

At the kitchen table he sat across from Chaské, who, in another smooth move, had taken the chair facing the door, as if by staring at it he thought he could escape. Tate brought them hot coffee and frybread, hung the cradleboard on the wall, and joined them. Baby Joe grabbed for the nearest cup, but before it could spill, Alex moved it out of reach and handed a piece of frybread to his son, who was teething.

Alex waited. Silence was normal while eating. Silence was useful while interrogating. If he started, Chaské would shift in his chair, look down and say nothing. He let his wife, nicknamed Question Box, start.

"Where've you been?" Tate asked. "Baby Joe doesn't have anyone else to play with."

Chaské held Baby Joe's arms as he stood up to be bounced. "Around."

Alex waited for more, then said, "That's a nice Harley you found."

"Where'd you get it?" asked Tate, reaching for Baby Joe, who wanted to nurse.

While she opened her blouse and Chaské looked away, Alex said, "Only bootleggers keep old Harleys to trade."

Chaské put down his coffee and looked directly at him. "You just miss me chopping firewood and building sweats - for free. Now I got a job."

"Where?" asked Tate.

Chaské hesitated. "In town."

There were no jobs in Eagle Nest for teenagers until June when TWEEP, the Tribe's summer youth program, started. Alex said, "You been hanging around them High Pine girls."

"No, I—" Chaské stopped.

"Who gave you the motorcycle?" asked Tate.

"I earned it!" Chaské pushed back his chair and stood up. "I don't have to answer your questions." He glared at Alex. "It's your own brother who gave me a job."

Zack, his half-brother, who was building a rival camp on Turning Hawk land up in the pines. Separate from the American Indian Movement and Camp Crazy Horse. So Zack had wooed Chaské with money, stealing the youngest of the AIM warriors for his own plans.

"Is it an interesting job?" asked Tate, handing a sleepy Baby Joe back to Chaské.

Alex smiled. Clever of her to keep him from leaving before he could shame Chaské for deserting his vows.

Chaské's eyes sparkled. "Yeah. First I learned to pitch a tipi. Now I'm building a Mon-go-lian yurt. From Asia. It's round and high with a solid wood floor. Better than a tipi."

"You're going to move into a Mongolian yurt?" asked Tate.

Alex could tell Chaské hadn't thought about leaving his pony in the corral or his small tipi at the Sundance grounds, let alone his commitment to the Great Mystery.

"No. It's too big." Chaské handed Baby Joe back to Tate, stood and spread his arms wide. "Bigger than this cabin. It's a meeting hall, for dances—"

Different from the old-time dance halls Alex had seen as a child, eight-sided log buildings for the forbidden sacred dances, forgotten and fallen in now, overgrown with snakeroot bushes. All they had left was the yearly Sundance, and as their leader, he must keep it a-going.

Chaské walked towards Alex. "You could build one, too, for AIM. I know how."

Alex stood up and shook his nephew's shoulders. Chaské had pledged four years of his life to seek a vision and to Sundance. "You must come back to the sweat lodge and prepare for *hanblechia*. You did good your first year, saw a sacred vision. This year you'll learn more."

Chaské looked down toward his biker boots. "Zack only has me to carpenter. I can't let him down."

Alex tightened his grip. It was the Great Mystery that Chaské couldn't let down. He was so young, he'd never seen what could happen. "I'll pay what you owe him for the cycle."

Chaské twisted out of Alex's grip and drew himself tall. "I already earned it. It's mine!"

"Then stay away from Zack," Alex shouted. "For shame, remember your sacred vows!"

But Chaské wasn't listening. He'd already stomped outside, revved the cycle's engine and left in a whirlwind of oil and exhaust.

Baby Joe woke from the racket. Alex took his son from Tate and rocked him in his arms for comfort. He'd do his best to keep his son safe, but he'd failed to reach his nephew Chaské.

Tate said, "I'll see if I can bring him back. But what will happen if he won't?"

WHY I WRITE

I WRITE to share a world no longer with us.

I write to honor the elders, record the passing of a culture, share the loss and encourage its retrieval. I write to show the young ones that a lost culture can be revived through storytelling to bind and heal. Even far from the Land, native values can be lived.

I've been blessed to live in times when only Lakota was spoken, when Honor meant doing things right—via feasts and memorial dinners, when anyone who came to the camp left with a handmade gift. We lived close to the Earth and appreciated the Creator's gifts: water life and air.

It is as if the elders have spoken in my sleep, asked not to be forgotten. Sometimes it is not my voice. I am merely a "translator" as the Spirit moves through my heart into my typing hands.

Dorothy Black Crow
dorothyblackcrow.com
dorothyblackcrow@gmail.com

DOROTHY BLACK CROW

AWARD-WINNING POET, memoirist, fiction writer and former professor of literature at Oglala Lakota College and the University of Michigan, author Dorothy Black Crow explores the reality of life on the Pine Ridge Reservation in the 1970s raising a sacred herd of buffalo. Married to a Lakota Sundance leader, she writes from a blend of understanding, experience, and knowledge.

Made in the USA
Middletown, DE
16 November 2019